Re-dis...
kii

THE MINERVA CLUB

CLUB

Victor Canning

This edition published in 2020 by Farrago,
an imprint of Duckworth Books Ltd
13 Carrington Road, Richmond, TW10 5AA, United Kingdom

www.farragobooks.com

By arrangement with the Beneficiaries of the Literary Estate of Victor Canning

'The Trojan Crate' first published as 'Escape for a lucky dog'
in *Today*, March 1963
'Flint's Diamonds' first published as 'To Lottie with love'
in *Today*, January 1963
'The Ransom of Angelo' first published as 'Twinkle, twinkle'
in *Argosy*, November 1961
'A Stroke of Genius' first published in *Ellery Queen's Mystery Magazine*,
February 1965
'Three Heads are Better than One' first published as 'With love from the boys'
in *Today*, April 1963

Ebook ISBN: 9781788422680
Print ISBN: 9781788422697

With grateful acknowledgment to John Higgins

Have you read them all?

Treat yourself again to the first Victor Canning novels –

Mr Finchley Discovers His England
A middle-aged solicitor's clerk takes a holiday for the first time and meets unexpected adventure.

Polycarp's Progress
Just turned 21, an office worker spreads his wings – an exuberant, life-affirming novel of taking your chances.

Fly Away Paul
How far could you go living in another's shoes? – an action-packed comic caper and love story.

Turn to the end of this book for a full list of Victor Canning's early works, plus – on the last page – the chance to receive **further background material**.

Contents

Introduction

Very little of Canning's work was straightforwardly humorous, but a good deal of it, both books and stories, could be called whimsical. The Minerva Club stories are a glimpse of what he might have achieved in the genre of pure comedy.

The Minerva Club of Canning's creation is a London club for criminals, reminiscent of the Junior Ganymede Club for butlers and valets that Jeeves belongs to in P.G. Wodehouse's stories. The entry qualification for the Minerva Club is to have served a prison sentence of two years or more.

Of course all the members are 'nice' criminals; we meet no murderers, rapists, or paedophiles here. Nor would any member steal from another member on club premises. "You could leave your wallet in your overcoat pocket in the cloakroom and find it there hours later" we learn in 'The Ransom of Angelo', and in the next story, 'Flint's Diamonds', this has escalated into: "You could leave your wallet on the edge of a hand basin and find it there a month later".

Shop talk is forbidden except after six o'clock in the smoking room, and unseemly conduct, such as brawling, leads to instant expulsion, as the Head brothers find out in the last story. It is the same basic joke as Wodehouse's, a club with all the relevant facilities and rituals that belong with a 'gentleman's club' but having members who were certainly not gentlemen.

The basic pattern of each story is a criminal venture going wrong but leading to an unexpected happy outcome for at least one of the participants. There is real ingenuity in the plotting and amiability in the characters, and the style in which the tales are told is that of a first-rate raconteur. I do not know if Canning ever intended to write a book's worth of Minerva Club stories, but the five stories that he finished make a delightful collection.

There is a tantalising hint that he might have written or at least planned a sixth story in the series. At the beginning of 'The Ransom of Angelo' we learn that Horace Head "had swiped the whole of the fruit and vegetable exhibits of a Royal Horticultural Society Exhibition. But that, too, is another story …"

After years of researching I have failed to find the sixth story, so I am fairly sure it does not exist, but I would love to be proved wrong.

John Higgins

The Trojan Crate

As Milky Waye, the secretary of the Minerva Club, was fond of saying, of all the members of the Club there was not one who could come up to Dog Downey for sheer goodness of heart. But as far as intelligence went, Dog was a long way from the top class. Mostly he worked in a minor capacity for other members of the Club. The only thing he did on his own was dog stealing—what might be called dognapping—at which he was an acknowledged master. Downey loved and understood dogs more than he did any creature, four- or two-legged. He could do anything with them.

Downey was a short, ugly man with a great mop of brown hair that fell forward across his face and gave him a shaggy look. Women, seeing him coming, would cross the road—which was a great pity for Downey had the utmost respect for women, though he had long reconciled himself to his bachelor state. At the age of twenty he had qualified for membership in the Club—no member is admitted to the august halls in Brook

Street unless he has done at least two years in one of Her Majesty's Prisons.

At the time of this story Downey had just completed a rewarding piece of work. He had stolen a valuable litter of four six-month-old Alsatian pups from a van which was delivering them to Cruft's Dog Show, and he had trained them until they were reliable house dogs and then sold them through an agent of his to various clients at fifty guineas apiece. Each time Downey parted with a dog it was like a sailor's farewell to his bride.

He came into the Minerva Club four days after this, his face as long as a fiddle with all its strings broken. We tried to cheer him up with brandy but it didn't work. In the end Maxy Martingale offered to take him in on a scheme he had just worked out. You should have seen the light in Downey's eyes at the thought of working with the great Maxy.

Maxy Martingale was brilliant. He was a tall, distinguished man who dressed like a City banker, had a voice like an archbishop, and the charm of a matinée idol. Dog Downey instantly became one of his men and Downey's warm heart overflowed at Maxy's kindness.

Maxy's scheme was simple, brilliant with the polish of genius, and cheap to operate. Maxy would choose a wealthy house where there was silver, paintings, an easy safe to crack or a fine collection of jewels to pick up—on the outside Maxy moved in good society and was well-informed—and then wait until he knew the owners were away for the night and the place manned only by the house staff. At about half-past five in the afternoon a van would draw up outside the house and a trio of Maxy's men would deliver a large packing case with the label of some big firm on it. The boys would dump the crate in the hall, get a servant to sign for it, and then be off. While the servant was walking around the crate wondering what was inside, the telephone would ring.

This would be Maxy, apologetic, anxious, smooth as silk, pretending to be an executive of the firm asking if the case had been delivered. Yes, it had. Oh, dear, how unfortunate and annoying—because a mistake had been made in addressing the crate and. it was not intended for Mr. So-and-So at all. Regrettably, it was too late now to get the van men to collect it. Would it be terribly inconvenient if the crate stayed there for the night? The van men would pick it up first thing in the morning.

And, of course, Maxy's charm worked and it always was convenient. And inside the crate, of course, would be one of Maxy's men. He would stay there until the house settled down for the night, then he would unfasten the crate, come out, lift the items listed by Maxy, pack himself and the loot back in the crate, screw it up from inside, and the next morning be whipped away by the returning van men before any loss had been discovered by late-rising servants taking advantage of their employer's absence.

Dog became Maxy's crate man—and he did the job well, no complaints, and made himself more money than he had seen for years. He even bought a new suit, got himself a haircut regularly, and began to bathe daily.

They did a couple of jobs in London, then worked the provincial towns for a few months, and finally came back to do another job in London. Maxy picked the house of a rich stockbroker who had a famous collection of gold and silver snuffboxes for which Maxy knew the right market. Duly at halfpast five, Dog was delivered— labelled *Fragile: Handle With Care*—to a house just off Hyde Park and dumped on the hall floor. A few minutes later, Dog heard the telephone ring and a servant answer it, and he knew that it was Maxy doing his stuff. The servant hung up, shuffled round the crate, gave it a nosey tap or two, and then moved away.

Dog sat inside and, an old hand now, patiently waited for time to pass. He used to amuse himself during this period by working out the possibilities from mating one breed of dog with another. On this particular night he was working on the problem of crossing a Portuguese Water Dog and a Staffordshire Bull Terrier, and time flew.

Eventually a clock in the hall struck midnight. Dog opened his thermos, had a cup of tea and a sandwich, and then, slipping on his gloves, he began to unscrew the crate. Five minutes later he was out. There was one shaded light burning at the foot of a curving marble stairway and the hallway was hung with tapestries and pictures. Dog brushed himself down, tidied his new haircut, and proceeded to work. He was well briefed on the layout. He went across the hall and into a study. In a little burglar-proof glass case was the collection of snuffboxes.

Dog fixed the alarm and lifted the snuffboxes, wrapping each one carefully in tissue paper, and putting the lot into a velvet cloth bag. It was no more than twenty minutes work. He went back to the crate and dropped his cloth bag into it. He was just about to get inside himself when a noise from the marble stairway made him turn round. The noise was a familiar, almost beloved one to him. It was the first low inquiring growl of an Alsatian demanding an invitation card or else.

Coming slowly down the stair was a plumpish, rosycheeked woman of about thirty-odd, her dark hair done up in curlers, wearing a faded purple dressing gown. Dog put her down as a housekeeper or a cook. At her side was a large black Alsatian with a small white spot on its forehead, and Downey placed the dog immediately. Once he'd seen a dog he never forgot it, and he recognized this as one of the litter he had stolen a few months before.

Recognizing the dog took some of the apprehension out of Downey. At least, he would have no trouble there. This was Sarah whom he personally had trained. He blessed the coincidence which had placed this, particular Alsatian in this house.

The woman, without a word, came slowly down the stairs and across to Dog, staring at him with a far-away, puzzled look—as though she couldn't believe her eyes. The dog kept close to her side.

Dog Downey, always polite to women, and rather pleased that this one hadn't winced at the sight of his face, said, "Good evening, ma'am."

"Gooda evening. You looka for something?"

Now Dog Downey was no fool. Here was the cook or the housekeeper and from her voice he guessed that she was Italian, and Dog knew that all foreigners were simple souls when it came to understanding English ways.

"That's right, ma'am," he said. "I was passing and just dropped in to see Mr. Whitlow. Old friend of mine." Whitlow was the name of the stockbroker who owned the house.

The woman nodded and said, "Issa good of you, Signore— but Signor Vitlow, not here tonight."

"A pity. I thought we might have a noggin together."

"Noggin—whata that?"

"A drinka ..." Dog made the motion of drinking and felt completely relaxed. The dog he could deal with— and the woman was a simple Italian who would believe anything. All he had to do was to keep things nice and friendly, take care of the woman somehow, and get out of the house with the snuffboxes. There could be no waiting for the crate to be collected in the morning— not this time.

"A drinka …" The woman smiled. "I show you. Thissa way."

She turned and went across to the back of the hall, the dog at her side cocking an inquiring eye at Downey who followed. A few moments later they were both at a table in the servants' sitting room with some bottles of beer in front of them.

"You're the cook here?" asked Downey.

"Thassa right. Only one month I come from Milano."

"I come from the Old Kent Road—I know what it's like to be in a strange place without friends," said Downey. "Here, let me fix that." He reached out for the beer and glasses and began to prepare the drinks.

Now it should be explained at this point that, although Downey had changed his line of operations, like a true professional he would never have dreamt of going outside his own house without all the adjuncts of a dog snatcher. After all, who could tell at what moment opportunity might not knock in the shape of a pedigreed Doberman Pinscher looking for a new owner. Downey always carried a knockout pill which could be fed to, say, a reluctant Great Dane. He fished now in his pocket for the pill and slipped it into the woman's drink. In five minutes she would drop off and Dog could safely depart—with the loot.

It must be said for Downey that he didn't like doing it to a woman. He was the last man to treat any woman like a dog—but it had to be done. He raised his glass and she drank with him, and his conscience troubled him. She was such a mice soul, friendly, with big peach-bloom cheeks and a dreamy look in her eyes as though she were still in Italy among friends who loved her, not here in cold, rainy London.

"Birra," she said, "very good. But vino issa better." As she put her glass down, she went on, "Tella me—you always weara gloves like that?"

Dog nodded. "Always." To leave fingerprints about in his work was like leaving a visiting card.

"Is very much gentleman to weara gloves. I lika that."

Dog nodded again, and then said, "What's your name?"

"Rosa," she said. "Rosa Caramaggio. Whassa your name?"

"Albert," said Dog truthfully, and then added untruthfully, "Brown."

"Issa nice. Alberto … Alber … Alb …" Her head began to drop and then with a last warm smile she flopped back into the wickerwork armchair and began to snore gently. Dog didn't mind the snoring. It always had that effect on dogs, too.

He sat and gave her a few moments, thinking to himself what a nice creature she was and how lucky he had been to meet someone so out of touch with the world of reality that she thought Mr. Whitlow's friends called long after midnight and got in without opening the front door.

When Rosa was sound asleep, Dog turned to deal with the Alsatian who, during all this, had been sitting between him and Rosa awaiting instructions.

Dog didn't try to rush it. Relations had to be established again.

"Well, now, Sarah, me old darling. Nice to see you. Remember Dog? Remember your old daddy, Dog?"

Dog gave a low whistle and Sarah pricked her ears forward, cocked. her head on one side, and was obviously making an effort at memory. Dog went on talking to her, giving her the dog patter of which he was a master. He had no doubts of winning Sarah over, and a few moments later, judging the time to be right, he started to stand up.

The first movement from him brought Sarah to all four feet. Her hackles went up and a growl came from her as though she were trying to imitate Etna in eruption. Dog sat down quickly. He was puzzled but not dismayed. He had not established complete recognition, that was all. He gave Sarah some more soft talk and she took it like a lady, relaxed, sitting back on her haunches.

But the moment Dog made another attempt to move, she was on her feet, hackles up again, and a row of fangs showing that would have sent Little Red Riding Hood into a dead faint. They did something for Dog Downey, too. They stimulated him to an effort of cerebration which finally gave him the answer.

Sarah clearly was having none of Dog's blandishments, and for a good reason that Dog now realized sadly.

Dog had never been double-crossed by any of his dogs before and it was a blow. Sarah just didn't recognize him because he was wearing a new suit and had had his hair cut. He might talk like Dog Downey, but he didn't look like Dog Downey, and because of his new bathing habits he didn't smell like Dog Downey—and Sarah was taking no chances. So there was Dog stuck with the dog.

And in the armchair Rosa Caramaggio snored gently, smiling in her sleep. And there the whole matter might have rested until morning when the outside staff arrived—except that Fate, which can be as tricky as a terrier if you hand it the wrong word, decided that Dog had already had more luck than he deserved. Fate now decided to do a little hounding. Sitting there, wondering what he could possibly do, and not dreaming of tangling with Sarah's fangs, Dog suddenly became aware of a burning smell. The door from the servants' sitting room into the kitchen was half open. Dog saw a trickle of blue smoke curling around the side of it like a lost genie looking for some wish to grant.

Instinctively he jumped to his feet, and instinctively Sarah was on hers and waiting for one more move. Dog sat down smartly and now he heard the faint whickering noise of flames. He had a situation on his hands. He could sit there and roast, and Sarah and Rosa would roast with him. But he would roast first because he was the nearest to the kitchen door.

Sweat breaking out on his ugly face, Dog decided that he would have to do something, no matter how desperate—a woman's life was at stake and that brought out all the Galahad in him. Behind him, in his chair, was a cushion. He carefully slipped it around and onto his knees. Sarah made no objection to movements performed while he sat. She just didn't like him on his feet.

Dog undid the fasteners on the cushion and pulled out the inner pillow He put the pillow on his left arm and knotted it into place with his tie—ruefully, because the tie was new like his suit.

Then he looked Sarah straight m the eyes and said, "Okay, old lady, you asked for it, so it's going to be rough—for you, I hope, not for me."

He leaned forward and opened another bottle of beer and poured it into a glass, while Sarah watched with interest. Then he suddenly jerked the beer into Sarah's face. At the same time he came to his feet and went for her, his padded left arm held in front of him like a shield.

Sarah lunged for him through a shower of pale ale, her fangs flashing and a battle growl rumbling in her throat. Her teeth went into the pillow and for a moment she hung from his arm. Dog jerked up his knee, slammed it into her unprotected belly, and Sarah went down in a heap.

In that moment Dog was on top of her and slipped the empty cushion cover over her head, twisting it tightly round her neck, muzzling and gagging her. He lifted her and ran quickly into the hall. Thanks to Maxy's briefing, he knew his way about the house as though he had lived there for years. By the front door was a small cloakroom. He kicked open the door, threw Sarah in, and then slammed the door shut on her.

He ran back across the hall, slipped on the marble tiling, slid five yards, cracked his head against the wall, and was a few seconds recovering. By the time he got back into the servants' sitting room, a great sheet of flame was roaring out through the kitchen door and little flames were flickering up and down the carpet and table cloth.

Dog grabbed Rosa, pulling her forward, and tried to lift her over his shoulder. But she was too heavy for Dog. He hadn't a hope of being able to carry her. So he did the next best thing. He slid her to the floor, grabbed her ankles, and, blinded and coughing from the smoke that now filled the place, he dragged her across the room on her. back, out into the corridor, and along to the hall.

Dog stopped beside a small table with a telephone and hurriedly put through a call to the Fire Brigade. Then, with the fire roaring away in the kitchen and the servants' sitting room, he decided that it would not be safe to leave Rosa in the hall. He tried the front door but this was locked and no key was visible. But next to the door he found a pair of French windows leading to a side garden.

He put his shoulders to these and burst them open. Then he went back, took his velvet bag from the crate, grabbed Rosa by the ankles, and dragged her into the garden. She would be quite safe there.

His duty done, all his chivalrous instincts satisfied, Dog now began to think of himself. He didn't want to be around when the fire engine arrived, and he didn't want to set off through the night streets of London carrying a bag of swag. Any policeman just seeing Dog out so late would stop him on general principles. So Dog thrust the bag deep into the heart of a little yew tree for subsequent collection and then took to his heels. Turning the corner of the street at a gallop, the inevitable happened—he ran into a policeman. The officer's hand shot out and grabbed Dog.

"Hullo, Dog—where are you off to in such a hurry?"

"Home," said Dog—without hope.

"Not tonight," said the policeman, confirming Dog's pessimism. And Dog was taken to the station and booked for loitering with intent to commit a felony. His protest to the station sergeant that the last thing he was doing was loitering went unheeded.

Dog spent the night in a cell and was left kicking his heels and threatening the Habeas Corpus Act until eleven o'clock the next morning. Then he was hauled up in front of a Detective-Inspector, an old friend of his.

"Okay, Dog," said the Inspector, "you'd better come clean. The crate trick is finished and we want to know who is running it. Not you, because you haven't the brains."

"What crate trick?" asked Dog. The Inspector sighed. "Last night it was worked on the house of a Mr. Whitlow. A collection of valuable snuffboxes is missing. Unfortunately for you a fire broke out while you were there, so you couldn't risk sitting in your crate and waiting for the usual morning collection. You broke out through the French windows—out, Dog, because the glass on the terrace and the way the catch was smashed prove it. Talk."

"I wasn't going to," said Dog innocently, "because I don't like being immodest—but I didn't do no such thing. I was walking down the street when I saw the glare of fire through the house windows. I went into the garden, found the French windows burst open—so I hopped in and telephoned for the Fire Brigade. Any responsible citizen would have done the same. Then I thought there might be someone about in danger, so—"

"So you rescued the cook, eh?"

"That's right. If anyone was pulling a crate job they must have done it before I arrived."

"Indeed? According to the police doctor this cook was given a knockout pill. The kind used for dogs. She must have caught you on the job. You gave her the old malarkey—she's a simple soul—and then you took a glass of beer with her and slipped her the Mickey Finn."

"To a woman? I would never do such a thing!"

"We'll see—they have just brought her down for questioning. She'll recognize you."

Dog's heart sank. A few moments later Rosa Caramaggio was brought into the room, and Dog resigned himself to the inevitable.

The Inspector said to Rosa, "Have you ever seen this man before?" Rosa looked at Dog and then shook her head. "Thissa man? No—I never see him."

"Not in Mr. Whitlow's house last night?"

"No. Never see thissa man before. Issa nice man?"

"Not very," said the Inspector sharply. "But— listen. This is the man who saved your life last night when the fire broke out. But I want to know what happened before the fire—when you caught him in the house—"

"Is thissa the man who save me!" Rosa cried. "Is a splendido man! Rosa always grateful!" She came forward and embraced Dog fervently, and Dog, delighted, but not knowing why she was helping him, said over his shoulder to the Inspector, "She was sleeping heavily when I rescued her. Probably uses sleeping pills."

"Break it up," said the Inspector. And that was it.

Try as he might, the Inspector simply could not shake Rosa. She had never seen Dog before, but her heart was overflowing with gratitude to him.

In the end the Inspector had to let Dog go, and off he went taking Rosa with him.

They walked down the road together to a small café and Dog ordered coffee and Chelsea buns; and while they waited for them, he gave Rosa a wink.

"You're a good un," he said. "Never seen me before. You should have seen the Inspector's face."

"But issa true," said Rosa.

Dog looked at her in amazement.

"But we had beer together in the sitting room. You came down the stairs with the dog—don't you remember?"

"No, I not remember."

"But," insisted Dog, "you came down with the dog. We had some beer and chat—"

"Oh!" Rosa put her hands to her mouth. "I dida that?"

"You certainly dida."

For a moment Rosa hesitated. Then leaning forward she said, "You keep a secret?"

"Anything for you, Rosa."

And then she explained that she was a confirmed sleepwalker, particularly when she had some worry, on her mind, and that night she had gone to sleep worrying. In her sleep the answer to her worry had come. She had left some underclothes to dry in front of an electric fire in the kitchen. So she had sleepwalked downstairs to remove them for fear of fire and …

"When I walka like that, *caro mio,* I talka, drinka, do everything like awaka—but afterwards I remember nothings. Speaka me—you married man?"

"No," said Dog, gazing with reverence at this splendid creature who did not avert her eyes at the sight of his face. "Bachelor."

But it was a state that did not last for long. They were married and eventually they had a son called Angelo—which is another story and one you may or may not have heard.

Flint's Diamonds

The Minerva Club—of which most people have never heard—is in a turning off Brook Street which, as you probably know, is very handy for the Ritz. It is a very exclusive club, chiefly because its membership is restricted to those who have served at least a two years' prison sentence and are able—beg, borrow, or steal—to pay yearly dues of £50.

Outside the club, the members are free to carry on their professional activities without any fear of being expelled—no matter what trouble they get into. But inside, there is nothing but good manners and the most honourable behaviour. You could leave your wallet on the edge of a hand basin and find it there a month later. In other words, an oasis of tranquillity after the cutand-thrust of the outside world where every man is for himself. The membership includes some distinguished names from the criminal calendar—Milky Waye, the Club's Secretary; Solly Badrubal, Chairman of the Wines Committee; Jim O'Leary, Treasurer—others including Horace Head, Marty

Martin, Dig Sopwith—dozens of them. And Flint Morrish.

This story is about Flint. He was one of the nicest men ever to have done time. He had a wooden leg—the result of something that went wrong with the gelignite in an early safe job; he had a beaming country-squire kind of face and an incurable faith in human nature—particularly in the female side of it.

Flint was always looking for the perfect woman—and always being disappointed. In romantic affairs he was as shortsighted as his own eyes—and he did nothing about either defect. He wouldn't wear glasses and he wouldn't learn by experience.

His latest "little number" was a blonde perfection, weighing about a hundred and ten pounds, somewhat top-heavy in her physical distribution, and with a pair of blue eyes that were like sultry lagoon pools. She came into the ring listed as Lottie Larson, age twenty-eight (unsubstantiated by any birth certificate). And Flint was gone on her. For him she was the woman, and for her he was the man—as soon as he could, no matter how, produce a properly authenticated bank balance of £10,000.

At the time of this story, Flint had about £5,000—which was high for him—and he was working on the balance. In fact, although he had taken Lottie on holiday to a small seaport town in Hampshire called Brankfold, Flint never missed a chance to pursue his calling—

Flint was a man who always had both eyes open for the slightest tip of the head from Opportunity.

One day, driving by himself—Lottie had stayed in the hotel with a headache—he passed a large country house just in time to see a man and a woman and two children drive out of the main gates. Flint stopped up the road and then wandered back to the house. He went, round to the servants' entrance and knocked. If there had been any reply he would have tried to sell the cook a complete set of the *Child's Wonder Book of Nature,* £14, delivered by post as soon as the cheque was cleared … But there was no answer to his knock.

So Flint went into the house through a convenient window, and wasting no time on reconnaissance he quickly found the study and the safe. It was a laughable safe to a man of Flint's experience. He opened it up with a collapsible jemmy (which he always carried with him), and found himself with about £50 in notes and a small wash-leather bag of uncut diamonds. At a quick and happy glance he knew the diamonds would be worth about £20,000 from any fence.

Flint drove back to his hotel whistling and found that Lottie, according to the hall porter, had recovered from her headache and gone off to the Pier Ballroom to a tea dance. Now Flint, because of his wooden leg, was not much of a dancing man. However, for Lottie's sake, he did his best. So he went after her, eager to show her the bag of diamonds.

Squinting around the ballroom, he finally picked out her blonde topknot. She was dancing with a man who, as far as Flint could see, was just a tall length of Donegal tweed with a black thatch on top.

Flint pushed his way across to them on the floor and took Lottie by the arm. It should be mentioned here that Flint was by nature a very jealous man where his "perfect women" were concerned—even though Flint knew that there were some limits to perfection.

Very politely Flint said, "Excuse me, the lady is tired," and started to lead his beloved away. But the face under the black thatch said to Flint, "The lady is not tired and is enjoying this dance with me. Stump off, you old pirate."

Now this was a most unfortunate thing to say to Flint. Flint didn't mind a bit being ribbed about his leg by members of the Minerva Club, but for any non-member even to show he had noticed it, let alone draw a crude allusion to it, was like putting a match to a powder keg.

Flint let go a roundhouse and put the man on the floor; but the man jumped up to an accompaniment of shrieks from the dancers and a drum roll from the band, and flashed over a quick right cross to Flint's jaw that dropped him to the floor as if he'd been shot. After that there was a few minutes of sharp give-and-take, during which Lottie disappeared, and then the police arrived. Flint and the other man were hauled off to the local police station—charge, disturbance of the peace.

Now on the way to the station Flint did some quick thinking. He knew that he would be up before the beak the next morning and he knew that with his record he would get at least a month—while the other fellow, such is justice, pleading he had been assaulted, would probably get off scot-free. The thought of a month didn't worry Flint much. In his profession the calendar was always coming up with such temporary blanks—but, of course, he was worried about the diamonds.

At the police station he was bound to be searched and his belongings taken. In the end Flint did what any intelligent monkey would have done: he pouched the small wash-leather bag inside his mouth up against his right cheek and all through the journey he sat with his hand against his face as though he had got a swollen jaw in the fight.

It worked in front of the desk sergeant. Flint was relieved of all his possessions and went mumbling into the detention cell.

The next morning he appeared before the judge and tried to mumble his way out of the charge against him. Maybe, if Flint could have spoken up clearly, the beak would have given him only a month; but the beak was a bit deaf and Flint's mumbles, though each one was over twenty carats in value, merely irritated him. Flint got a sentence of two months, and the other man was discharged.

Now the jail at Brankfold was a small one, adjoining the Chief Constable's house—all one building, in fact. There were only eight cells, and business in Brankfold was never enough to fill them all. Flint was given a top-floor cell with a view of the sky and nothing to look forward to except visiting day when he knew that Lottie would be around.

Flint was aware, of course, that while he had got away with the swollen-face gambit, he could not keep it up for two months. Fat jaws just do not last that long and somebody would get suspicious. So he decided to unpouch the diamonds, hide them, and only pouch them again on the day he left jail. Being a man of resource, he proceeded to unravel enough thread from his bed mattress to make a length of string. He tied the washleather bag to it, stood on his bed, and lowered the diamonds through the grille of the ventilator up in the corner near the ceiling, tying the other end of the string neatly and inconspicuously to the grille frame. Then he settled down patiently to do his two months. Sixty days and he would be out—with scads of money in the bank—and Lottie and bliss forevermore.

On the first visiting day he told Lottie about the diamonds and about the splendid future that lay before them. Her eyes turned to limpid pools which promised exotic delights. She began to describe the kind of house she would like to live in, and the colour she already fancied for the dining-room curtains.

Flint congratulated himself on his good taste in falling for a woman who was not only beautiful and shapely but such a magnificent home builder. The idea of home, it must be mentioned, was something very dear to Flint since he had never had one, having been found in a railway carriage when he was three and having flitted from then on through various institutions and remand homes to Borstal and, finally—the crowning achievement of his career—five years in Dartmoor. Yes, Flint was all for a home of his own—with his perfect woman.

But the next week, when Solly Badrubal came to see him, he was a bit shaken. "To tell a woman you have a packet of diamonds stashed away is folly, Flint—sheer folly. She could sell you out just for the reward she could get for the return of stolen property."

"Not Lottie—there is no such baseness in my Lottie."

"Then she's no woman."

"That," said Flint firmly, "is something I know to be untrue. Don't you worry about Lottie. Just you get hold of a good fence and tell him I'm coming out with a packet and to have the money ready. I don't want any delay in getting off on my honeymoon. Lottie is all for the Bahamas. She is going up to London next week to choose her outfit."

Well, all might have been smooth sailing. Lottie could have gone to the Bahamas with Flint, they could have been happy for as long as the money lasted—which is as much as any reasonable person can expect—but things went wrong.

At the end of the first month there was a fire in the kitchen quarters of the jail, and these were directly under

Flint's cell. He woke up one night to find his cell full of smoke, the floorboards like a hot plate, and before he could do anything, a couple of officious guards had come in and rescued him.

Flint was very annoyed with this prompt rescue—he'd been given no time to retrieve his diamonds. The fire was put out smartly, and Flint, for the rest of his time, was lodged in another cell—and never once did he get a chance to go back to his original cell.

Eventually he was released, empty-handed, and he came back to London to discuss his problem with some of the boys at the Minerva Club. And let it be said, here and now—when any member of the Club was in trouble, the others rallied round with advice and help and with only a minimum thought of selfinterest.

Well, there were several opinions offered. Solly Badrubal said, "Go back and get pinched again in Brankfold. Slug that same fellow—then maybe you'll be put back in the same cell they first gave you."

Flint shook his head. "When I left they hadn't even begun to repair it."

Milky Waye suggested that Flint try and get a job as a guard there. They could easily fake his credentials.

"They'd recognize him by his wooden leg," said Jim O'Leary.

Horace Head said, "You could bribe one of the warders to get the rocks for you."

No one took any notice of Horace.

So there was Flint in a curious predicament and the prospect of a bright future slowly tarnishing until one day Lottie came swaying on stiletto heels into the Ladies' Annexe of the Club, was settled with a large pink gin, and announced to Flint that she had the answer. Ever since leaving Brankfold, she said, she had subscribed to the *Brankfold Courier*.

"Why?" asked Flint.

"Because we had such a nice time there. I'm sentimental like that."

"Ah, yes," said Flint.

"And look at this," said Lottie. She placed a copy of that week's *Courier* in front of him. There on the front page was the story of how the Brankfold jail, so little used, had been declared obsolete by the Prison Commissioners and was to be put up for auction at the end of the month—the whole bloomin' business, Chief Constable's house, eight-cell block with kitchen and offices, and an exercise yard that could be converted into a nice garden.

"But I don't want to buy it," said Flint.

"You don't have to, darling. But they must let people look over the property—people who are thinking of buying. You just go down and get an order to view, get into that cell, and pinch back your diamonds."

Although it was strictly forbidden to indulge in such an act in the Ladies' Annexe, except on guest nights, Flint took Lottie in his arms, upset her pink gin, and gave her a resounding kiss.

The next day Flint was off to Brankfold with Solly Badrubal, Jim O'Leary, Horace Head, and Lottie. Flint had no intention of going into the prison himself—some of the staff were still there and might recognize him—and there was still a hullabaloo going on about the original theft of the diamonds. No, Flint was much too clever for that. They all stayed at the Royal Hotel. Solly tried his hand first. He got an order to view from the auctioneers.

When he came back he shook his head. "No luck, Flint. A young man came with me from the auctioneers. Couldn't shake him off—and he wasn't very keen even about me going into the cell. The floor's still unsafe."

The next day Jim O'Leary tried. But it was the same story. The auctioneer's young man had stuck to him like a leech and just couldn't be shaken off.

The next day, without much hope, they tried Horace. Horace came back beaming. "You know, it would make a nice place, that prison. Good garden. Nice young man from the auctioneer's told me it'll go for about ten thousand. A snip."

"What about my diamonds?"

"Oh, them. Well, I didn't fancy that floor. Even if I did, the young chap wouldn't leave me alone."

"Damn the fellow," said Flint.

Then he turned to Lottie, desperation stimulating an idea in him. Although Flint—out of chivalrous respect—never involved any of his perfect women in his professional schemes, this seemed a very special case. He said, "You must try, darling. You go over the place and when you get to that cell, you faint— calling out for water. He'll dash off and leave you alone for a minute or two—and that's all you need."

"What—faint on a floor that's unsafe?"

"Don't be silly. Faint in the door way. Anyway the floor will hold you."

Lottie hesitated for a moment, then she said, "All right, darling. It seems the only way left—and it means so much to us both."

"It means twenty thousand nicker," said Solly. "For that I'd go into a coma for a month."

So Lottie went off the next day and did her stuff. She came back upset, with a patch of burnt wood ash on her neat little rump, and said angrily, "It didn't work. I fainted, calling for water—and what do you think that fool of a young man did? He caught me up in his arms, pulled a brandy flask from his pocket, and damned near choked me. And when I said I wanted water, he carried me down into the kitchen. I couldn't shake him off. I've had enough of this diamond hunt, Flint. I'm going back to London and you can call me when you've got the diamonds."

And she left in a huff. Flint wasn't going to have his perfect woman unless he cracked his problem—and soon. Flint was a little upset but he saw her logic: you can't expect a perfect woman to hang around forever, waiting for a payday that never comes.

However, that evening in his bedroom the four of them got down to it over a bottle of whisky, and with the help of a telephone call to Milky Waye the problem was solved. They would go to the auction and buy the prison. Flint had £5,000— the rest, if necessary, could be raised after the sale on a mortgage. Once the prison was his he could get the diamonds the others taking a small cut for their help—and then Flint could resell the prison, maybe at a profit. It was Milky's idea. Milky said that he would come down and bid for Flint at the auction. Which he did.

The auction was held outside in the exercise yard of the prison and there were a lot of people there. As Flint said, "Who the hell wants to buy a prison? They must be mad." Only Horace answered. "You could make a nice place of it—nice garden."

"Shut up," said Jim O'Leary. "It gives me the creeps just being in this yard. Think of all the poor souls who've slogged around here, longing for a butt to smoke."

The bidding was brisk and went quickly up to £7,000. There it lagged a bit, then got its second wind, and, finally, Milky Waye had it knocked down to him at £11,000.

As the crowd dispersed, the auctioneer said to Milky Waye, "If your principal will just sign these papers … and give me his cheque for the deposit … Thank you. Here are the keys—we'll get the deeds and all that settled later. There may be a little delay because I'm short-handed at the moment—staff trouble, you know. Wonderful little property—full of possibilities …"

"Oh, full," said Milky.

Then the five of them stood about, waiting for the crowd to go, the bunch of cell keys in Flint's hands. When the last person had left, Flint stumped off toward the top cells with the others following him. He unlocked the door and held the rest back.

"Floor won't hold us all," he said, and then added with a grin, "Don't want any misfortune at the last moment, do we?"

But that was exactly what he got. He went gingerly over the floor and got up on the bed. The end of the string was still tied to the ventilator grille. He pulled it up—all two feet of it— and there at the other end was the wash-leather bag.

Flint jerked it free and went back to the others, who crowded round to see the diamonds. But already thunderclouds had gathered on Flint's face. The only thing in the bag was a large sheet of mauve notepaper, carefully folded and smelling of scent.

"No diamonds—I've been robbed!" stormed Flint.

"Perhaps you've got the wrong cell?" suggested Horace.

"Shut up." said Jim O'Leary. "Read the blasted letter," said Solly Badrubal, "though why should I be anxious for bad news?"

"It's a woman's writing," said Milky. "That's a bad sign."

"It's Lottie's," said Flint, and then more weakly, holding the letter out to Milky, "You read it—I can't …"

"You really should get some glasses," said Horace.

"Shut up," said Milky, and he began to read the note, which said:

Darling Flint,

I know this will distress you, but it is so much better to be honest and hurt a person than to be dishonest and store up unhappiness for us both. It is not just your wooden leg—after all, many a woman has truly loved a man with physical disabilities—

"This," said Milky, "was not composed by Lottie. It is not her style. She had help."

He went on:

—but it is rather your blemishes of character, particularly your quick temper, which have decided me.

I think I knew this from the moment you came to the tea dance and were so brutal to sweet Duncan Brown

"Who the hell," said Flint, "is Duncan Brown?"

"Search me," said Solly.

"I know," said Horace. "He's that tall, dark-haired chap who wears a Donegal tweed suit—the one from the auctioneer's office. We had a long talk together. Yes, Duncan Brown—that's his name."

Milky was saying, "Just listen to the rest of it—"

From that moment I knew you were not the man for me.

Duncan and I love each other—for a long time I was not sure, but when I fainted in here, meaning to do all you said, he was so kind and chivalrous, so wonderfully tender and understanding, that those few moments in his arms

"Enough!" roared Flint. "She's bilked me."

"They are," said Milky, finishing the reading of the note to himself, "honeymooning in the Bahamas. And I guess that's why the auctioneer is short-staffed."

Flint turned—a broken man and stumped away, saying, "I need a whisky. A very large one. And what the hell do I do now—with a prison on my hands?"

Well, of course, if life is full of disappointments, it also has its compensations. Nothing is so bad as it looks. In fact, in this case it was much better. Flint tried to sell the prison but never got a decent offer for it. In the end he converted it into a private hotel for "special" guests recuperating from misfortune or just wanting to be anonymous for a while. Most of them were members of the Minerva Club who wanted to get quietly away into the country, and all of them appreciated the irony of living comfortably in a converted jail.

Flint—with occasional help from Horace—made over the exercise yard into a garden, and discovered that he had green fingers, that he had no further longing for "the perfect woman," and that at last he had found a home which, not only in appearance but in association, was full of the rich memories of the past.

The Ransom of Angelo

Milky Waye, the secretary of the Minerva Club, once
figured out that if the combined prison sentences
served by the members of the club were laid end to
end, backwards, you'd finish up in the year 1066. As a
"numbers man," Milky could do almost anything with
figures and usually get away with it. His few failures,
however, added seven years to the Minerva's record for
total sentences.

The club itself, in a turning off Brook Street, had a
highly respectable and discreet appearance, a uniformed
porter at the desk (age sixty-five, with ten years of prison
service), and a membership of about three hundred. The
conditions of entry were that a member must be able
to contribute two years or more to the trip back to the
Battle of Hastings, and also be able to pay—or beg,
borrow, or steal—£50 a year as dues.

Outside, the club members were free to carry on their
adroit adaptations to the strains of modern civilization.
Inside the club, there was nothing but good manners and
the most honourable behaviour. You could leave your

wallet in your overcoat pocket in the cloakroom and find it there hours later. The place was an oasis of tranquillity after the stresses and strains of the workaday world. In the quiet of the smoking room, so conducive to speculative thought, some of the finest and most involved schemes for illegal profit had been worked out. It was here, for instance, that Flint Morrish had evolved the tactical plans which had made him the only ex-convict ever to own a prison. He still owned it—but that is another story, though it has something to do with this one.

In the smoking room Solly Badrubal had turned the loss of his wife's black poodle into the acquisition of a film company and the birth of a new child star, Angelo Downey. This story is about Angelo Downey and Solly Badrubal, but not about the poodle. There is a dog in this tale of the Minerva Club—a young Gordon setter puppy with a tail like a whipping hawser and a grin that flopped right down to its gawky knees.

The whole affair began with Milky Waye talking one day in the smoking room to Solly and Jim O'Leary who was just back from a trip to Devonshire and five years of brisk moorland air. Each was sitting behind a large whisky. Milky was a tall, distinguished-looking man with white hair, a little waxed moustache, and the kindly twinkle of a family lawyer in his eye. Solly was very short, very plump, very bald, and with a sleek quick kind of movement that made you think of those little jobs that wriggle out of the cracks behind baths—

silverfish, I think they are called. But he had a big heart of the brightest alloy right on his sleeve and a smile you couldn't see for cigar smoke.

Jim O'Leary was tall, dark, hard, and brooding, like a hellthreatening parson who liked his parsonage to be full of draughts and damp. He had no sense of humour at all. He'd thrown it away long ago as a hindrance.

Milky Waye said to Solly, "I see your new film is having its première next week."

"That is so," said Solly. "You should have two tickets. Five guineas each. It is a great story. The small boy torn between his divorced mother and father. He loves them both. It is full of heart. This mother, you see, is a striptease artiste, and we have a wonderful scene where she is doing her act and the father—he is a police inspector and he does not know she is doing this work to get more money for them to put down the deposit on a house—"

"Quite," said Milky. "It is disgusting how the police are underpaid. They would be better tempered, maybe, if they were decently paid."

"And this father," said Solly, "leads a raid on the place. And then—"

"It will make a lot of money?" asked Milky.

"It would make more," said Solly, "if I did not have to pay that curly-headed brat Angelo Downey so much. And what it does make will be milked by tax. I am a poor man through giving the public great pictures."

Milky nodded, and then after a pause said, "You know, despite the Finance Act of 1960, there is still a great body of legal opinion which holds that a subject is still entitled to arrange his financial affairs so that they do not attract taxation."

"As an accountant," said Solly, "you tell me a new angle. There ain't none I know of."

Jim O'Leary stirred and reached for his whisky. "There's always some new graft with Milky."

"Quite right," said Milky. "It would need three of us. Save you thirty thousand pounds. You cut me in for five, and Jim for five. I've been giving it a lot of thought."

Solly ordered three more whiskies and was silent until they came. "Expound," he said, "I am a reasonable man, but I do not like being an overtaxed man."

Milky Waye said, "You have this Angelo Downey child who is a public figure."

"He is also a public menace."

"Never mind. You have a big picture about to be shown. So the boy is kidnapped and held for ransom— say, forty thousand pounds. Jimmy and I arrange that. You pay over the money and the rest is easy."

"I am not quite following you, Milky. So I pay over the money?" Milky smiled. "We pay it back to you, but nobody knows this. So you are not out of pocket except for the ten thousand which we keep out of the forty. Now, you have had to pay forty thousand pounds to get Angelo Downey back. Safe and sound. He is a valuable asset to your company. The ransom money is a tax deductible expense. Forty thousand pounds on which you would have had to pay surtax means that you have saved yourself about twenty-six thousand pounds to begin with. And you also have thirty thousand back that no one knows about. So you have made yourself fifty-six thousand pounds tax free."

"It's complicated," said Jim.

"It's not strictly accurate," said Solly. "But it sounds interesting. Milky is dressing it up a little, but I do not mind that. Out of forty thousand pounds on which I would normally pay tax, I avoid tax altogether. I save, say, twenty-six thousand pounds. I pay you ten. I am left with a net saving of sixteen thousand pounds."

"It is another way of looking at it," said Milky equably.

"We will look at it that way," said Solly. "But sixteen thousand is sixteen thousand, and I am all for it. The only condition is that the boy is not hurt. I would personally like him hurt, but he is a business asset. Don't tell me nothing, but go ahead. And it is better done in the next few days for it will be wonderful publicity for the film. But he is an awkward brat, and sharp as a pair of shears. Also he is strictly dishonest and disrespectful as well as having a swollen head."

"I shall handle him," said Jim. "I am now against children since it was a small girl wandering down in the middle of the night for a drink of water who got me sent to the Moor this last time. She was curly-headed and wore

pink pyjamas with white rabbits on them and—" he held
out his right hand—"this scar is where she bit me when I
wanted her to stop shouting. I am against children."

So the kidnapping of Angelo Downey was arranged.
And for a hundred pounds' share in the project Milky
and Jim O'Leary brought in Horace Head—more as
a chaperone, or companion-and-nursemaid, and also
because they both trusted Horace. He was so dull-witted
that half the time he did not understand what was going
on and so could be a most confusing witness if he ever
got into the box.

In fact, Horace's engaging smile, loosely framed
by cauliflower ears, and his good-natured, oblique
conversational style had driven more than one London
magistrate to nearapoplexy. But he was fundamentally a
good egg, and was famous for the fact that in his early
days, when down on his luck as a fighter, he had swiped
the whole of the fruit and vegetable exhibits of a Royal
Horticultural Society Exhibition. But that too is another
story ...

Angelo Downey was fifteen, looked about twelve,
and had the mental equipment and temperament of a
fallen angel with no regrets for the past. He looked like
a miniature Italian tenor, dark, curly-haired, plump, with
sun-warm cheeks, sloe-black eyes, a flashing smile for the
public and cameras, and a permanent scowl at other times.

At the end of a day's work or devilry he liked to relax
with a large gin and bitter lemon and a cigar. He was

wilful, wayward, and unpredictable, and with all the natural wit of a boy born just off the Old Kent Road who had been working with his father as a dog stealer at the age of five. If he had one passion in life, it was dogs. He was capable of love only for dogs.

At eight o'clock on the evening of the première of his film, *The Model Mother,* he was sitting alone in his room at the Leroy Hotel, dressed in a dinner jacket, enjoying his gin and bitter lemon and cigar, and feeding crackers to a loosely co-ordinated Gordon setter puppy of some eight months. The puppy which had a gold and diamond-studded collar around its neck was called, according to a gold medallion which hung from the collar, Prince Narrowmeath of Moortown. Angelo referred to him as Bugs which the puppy seemed to prefer. Already the two were in love.

Half an hour before, Angelo had stolen the dog from a room at the far end of the corridor. The door has been slightly ajar and Angelo had seen Bugs sitting on a settee. He had whistled gently and the dog had come to him. As simple as that—except that the whistle had been one of the secrets of his father's trade.

There was a knock on the door and Solly Badrubal entered. He gave Angelo a precise good evening, took his gin and tipped it into a vase, and stubbed out the cigar.

He said, "One of the press boys has to see you this way and your future is ruined. Mothers do not like little boys to do these things."

"My mother does not mind. And I am not little. I don't want to go to this première. I want to stay here with Bugs."

"This animal? We should ring for it to be taken away. We do not want any more dog trouble."

"He followed me. Can I help it? Besides he's going to the première with me and on the publicity tour. Otherwise …" He shrugged his plump shoulders.

Solly considered this for a moment. After the première Angelo was being driven to the station to get a sleeper north for the beginning of a personal appearance tour. His bags had already been taken down to the waiting Rolls Royce which was to take him first to the première, then to the railway station. Since Milky Waye was the chauffeur, and Jim O'Leary and Horace Head were sitting in the back right now, Angelo would never reach the première.

Solly decided that they were capable of coping with a dog as well as Angelo, so he said, "It is okay. Small boy with a dog—it is a good touch. But after the première he goes back to his owner."

"He stays with me."

"You will be pinched for stealing. Even from here I can see that collar he wears is worth a ton."

Angelo nodded. "Easily. And he's worth about two hundred. I know the Narrowmeath of Moortown strain. Two of them have been Cruft's Champions."

"Go clean your teeth and rinse your mouth out. We do not want you blowing gin and cigar at the Duchess of Malmerton when you are introduced. You forget that all the takings on this show are for the Children of Fallen Mothers?"

"What do I care?" said Angelo as he went obediently to the bathroom followed by Bugs.

"Or me," murmured Solly. And then he called through the open bathroom door. "You will travel alone in the Rolls. Make the big entrance. I will come behind. You can give five autographs. No more. And watch what you write. There have been complaints which I have had to pay the press boys to hush up. Some of the things you write are just not nice."

Five minutes later Angelo, leading Bugs, went through the foyer of the Leroy and out to the waiting Rolls Royce. The pavement was thick with fans and a tall, spinsterish-looking woman with wired-up spectacles thrust an autograph book into his hands. He gave her a wan, world-worn smile, his eyes misting with easily controlled tears, and wrote, *I am really a dwarf, aged 40, with a wife and three children. They keep me drugged and won't let me see my family. Ring my wife at Whitehall 03472 and tell her. Angelo Downey*

He got into the car, beaming. Whitehall 03472 was Solly Badrubal's number.

The smile went from his face as he found himself flanked in the back seat by Horace and Jim. As the car drove off, Angelo said scowling, "What the hell are you doing here? I'm supposed to be alone." Through the half-glass partition he shouted to the chauffeur, "Stop and kick these men out."

Milky turned and said to Jim O'Leary, "Smack his head and tell him to shut up."

Jim nodded, cuffed Angelo, and said, "A pleasure. Already I do not like him."

Horace giggled gently and patted Angelo's shoulder saying, "Don't mind Jim. He ain't got no kids of his own. That's a nice dog. Joints want kind of screwing up a bit, eh? Take up the play on the bearings."

"What is all this?" asked Angelo.

"Kidnapping," said Horace happily. "Gonna make a lot of money out of you. No rough stuff, though—like cutting off ears. You'll like it. You know summat? You look kind of smaller than you do in your films. I seen 'em all."

"Belt up!" said Angelo.

"That's right," said Jim. "Belt up, Horace."

Milky turned his head and said pleasantly, "You sit tight, Angelo. Any trouble from you and they'll push you under the seat and put a blanket over you."

Angelo said nothing as the car turned over Waterloo Bridge. He pulled out a cigar case and selected one, trimming the end with a gold clipper.

Horace watched him fascinated, and said admiringly, "Your old man would certainly be proud of you. Regular little gent you've become. Fancy—old Dog Downey's boy! Sad when he passed away. Still, cigars is bad, you know. For the wind.

Got to keep fit." He banged his broad torso and the car echoed with a hollow sound.

"Muzzle him," said Angelo. And then to the back of Milky's head he said, "How much are you asking for me?"

Milky chuckled. "Forty thousand pounds. Satisfied?"

Angelo chuckled, too. "Solly will break a blood vessel. But it's good publicity. Where are we going?"

"Wait and see," said Jim, "and since you're smoking, what about handing 'em round."

Angelo hesitated for a moment and then with a shrug pulled out his case and selected two cigars which he handed to them. He watched them light up and settle back as the car purred luxuriously through the outer suburbs. Five minutes later the two cigars exploded in their faces.

Angelo leaned forward, resting his hands on top of Bugs's head, and laughed until the tears came. Jim brushed his waistcoat free of burning shreds and leaned over and smacked Angelo's head hard.

"Practical joker, eh? Maybe I should cut your ears off."

Angelo, still laughing, said, "Better not. You wouldn't get forty thousand then."

Horace held up the shattered stub of his cigar, frowning, puzzled, and said quietly, "Funny, ain't never had one do that before. Something must have got in the tobacco."

"Belt up," said Jim angrily. "If this little bleeder—"

"Quiet back there," called Milky.

Horace lay back beaming and said, "Know something? First time I been in a Rolls Royce. Nothing to it, is there? I could take this for days."

After about half an hour, when they were in the country, Angelo said suddenly, "I've been thinking. You could make it fifty thousand and cut me in for ten. Solly need never know. And for ten I'd cooperate."

From the front of the car Milky, without turning, said firmly, "For nothing you will cooperate."

Angelo just shrugged, and after a while he hauled Bugs up onto his lap and they both went to sleep.

Horace looked over them to Jim and said happily, "Nice sight, ain't it. Boy and his dog. All kids like dogs, you know. Kids got to have pets."

"If he should have a pet," said Jim, "it ought to be a snake. Cut him in for ten thousand! Where does he get these ideas?"

Ignoring him Horace went on, "Got to have a pet of some kind. Remember Flint Morrish and me, we had a couple of mice when we was in Parkstone. Very healthy, Parkstone, with all that sea air. They had a family. Not a hair on 'em. Pink as babies' bottoms. Wonder what happened to old Flint?"

"You'll see him tonight," said Jim. "That's where we're going."

There is a small town in Hampshire, a little port of about five thousand people called Brankfold. At one time the town had a small jail attached to the old stone house of the Chief Constable. But after a time the jail became so little used that it was decided to close it down and to sell the building. Flint Morrish, for reasons that don't belong to this story, bought it, and got stuck with it. But being a resourceful man with a wry sense of humour, he decided to convert it into a private hotel and take in carefully selected guests. Most of them were members of the Minerva Club who wanted to get quietly away into the country for a while, and most of them appreciated the irony of living in a comfortably converted jail.

The outside of the building had been left as it was—ironstudded doors, barred windows to all the cells, and a surrounding wall with a formidable *chevaux de frise*. If you don't know what that is, it doesn't matter—but never try to climb over one in the dark. In the former exercise yard Flint had made a nice little garden, with a lily pool and goldfish, and had settled down to living happily ever after. He had a wooden leg— the result of something going wrong with the gelignite in an early safe job—a beaming country-squire kind of face, a passion for loud tweeds, and the greenest fingers in the county. He loved flowers and they grew for him.

There were eight cells in the ex-jail and these had been doubled up to make four good-sized rooms. There were four other rooms in the house, and it was as private and secluded a place to keep Angelo Downey as Milky Waye could think of. There wasn't a ghost of a chance that he could break out so long as the main door was kept locked. And he wasn't going to be there long enough to finish a tunnelling job.

Angelo was installed with Bugs in one of the cells. It was a nice room with a pale-blue carpet, chintz at the barred windows, a four-poster bed, and a washing place behind a curtain.

For the first day of his kidnapping, Angelo was reasonably well-behaved. He spent most of the morning reading the newspapers which carried headline stories of his kidnapping and his career, then took Bugs for a walk around the small garden with Horace in attendance, and then lunched in his room.

Flint Morrish, having lunch with Milky and Jim, said, "Strikes me as a nice lad. Modest, no trouble."

Jim O'Leary said, "You wait."

That evening Angelo demanded a gin and bitter lemon to go with his cigar. Flint, old-fashioned about the training of children, refused him this. Ten minutes later Horace, sitting on guard outside Angelo's room, shouted, "Fire!"

They all rushed up to find that Angelo had set fire to the hangings of his bed and was sitting in a chair by the window, calmly smoking his cigar and watching his temporary home burn.

Flint was furious at the damage to his best hangings, but Angelo got his drink. He also, when his dinner was brought up, refused to eat it. Lamb chops and green peas didn't appeal to him. He wanted an omelette of which he was especially fond—a cheese omelette laced with potted shrimps and shredded pimento.

Flint, a home-loving man, was also a good cook and—anxious to preserve his property from further damage—finally allowed Angelo to come down to the kitchen and make the omelette. Angelo, whose mother was Italian, was a good cook. Flint and the others stood by while Angelo demonstrated his skill. The omelette completed, Angelo dined at the kitchen table and gave Flint some of the omelette to taste.

Flint rolled his eyes. "Delicious," he said.

"You like it?" Angelo's eyes beamed at Flint's appreciation. "If you wish I'll make some more for you all."

He made four omelettes for them, but at their first mouthfuls Flint and Jim jumped to their feet, roaring with fury, and grabbing for glasses of water. They turned on Angelo with murder in their eyes. He had, surreptitiously, emptied a full can of mustard powder into the omelettes. Milky, who had cautiously delayed touching his omelette, got between Angelo and the two men.

"No violence. Remember. He's good money unmarked. But mark him and he'd be left on the shelf in a clearance sale. You ought to have known better than trust him."

At which point Horace, still eating at table, looked up and said, "What's all the fuss? Best omelette I ever had. Minds me of a curry my old lady used to make. Put a

61

thirst on you for a week. Nothing wrong with a thirst if you've got the money—"

"Belt up!" roared Jim.

"Take him up to his room," said Flint quietly. "Take him up to his room." The colour had gone from his ruddy squire's cheeks and he was rapping the end of his wooden leg against the floor in an angry tattoo.

The kidnapping arrangement was that in four days' time Solly Badrubal would send one of his clerks with the ransom money to Southampton where Flint would meet the man in a café. At first, Solly had only wanted to send the £10,000 due to Milky and Jim—out of which they would pay Horace £100, and Flint £500 for the use of his house.

But Milky had pointed out that since Solly's clerk would be an honest man he would spot that there was only £10,000. All the papers had blazoned the sum of £40,000, and the risk of the discrepancy leaking out could be dangerous. Reluctantly, Solly had agreed to send the full amount.

But before the four days had passed, all the men—and especially Flint—had had some very bad moments with the ingenious-minded Angelo. The boy was allowed the freedom of the garden, and to pass the time he took to training Bugs to fetch and carry things. He'd walk the setter around teaching it to carry a bag or newspaper, make it fetch a ball, come back, sit, and drop the ball at the command of word or whistle. Naturally, both boy and dog got bored at times with lessons, and then they would get the wind up their tails and go romping all over the place.

Flint's flowers suffered. Bugs dug holes in the lawn and rockery, and quite a few of the garden dwarfs had their heads knocked off. The survivors had black moustaches pencilled on them.

Apart from all this Angelo was an incorrigible practical joker. In one of the suitcases which had come with him he had enough booby traps and tricks to stock a "magic" store. All four of the men suffered. The details of their suffering are unimportant—they suffered. But the refrain—from Angelo— which went with it left them cold. He would co-operate if they cut him in on a share of the ransom.

They were prepared to suffer almost anything rather than cut him in. Even Horace, who took a long time to notice things, began to feel that there was something add about the house. Every time he put his hand on the doorknob to go into Angelo's room he got an electric shock. He complained to Flint about faulty wiring and got a short answer.

Before two days had passed Flint was shattered—by the state of his house and beloved garden, and appalled at the thought that he was only going to get £500. On the second night, after some thought, he telephoned a friend of his who was a sea captain working a small cargo ship out of Southampton. From then on, Flint faced Angelo's demolition work with a certain amount of resignation …

Two days later, when Flint returned from his rendezvous in Southampton, he informed the others that the messenger with the money hadn't turned up. Milky Waye telephoned Solly Badrubal and was indignantly told that Solly had sent off the money, even seen the man on the train. Solly, panicking, wanted to know what was going on down there. Milky Waye, suffering from a cold from opening a door and having a bucket of water fall on him, sneezed violently into the phone, and telling Solly to keep his hair, on, added grimly that he'd have to look into things.

Back in the kitchen he questioned Flint about the messenger. "Flint, you aren't pulling a fast one, are you?"

"Not me," said Flint. "But that messenger is. I'll take a hundred to one on it. He comes down with the money and gets the first boat out of Southampton. Never see him again. It's what we'd all think of, isn't it?"

"It is," said Jim. "But this guy was from Solly's office. A little clerk chap. He wouldn't have that kind of mind."

"Maybe it developed on the train, hugging all that loot," said Flint evenly. "He's on his way to South America now. Never see him again."

Which was true, of course, for Flint had arranged it with his captain friend at the price of a couple of hundred quid. But the clerk didn't have the money. Flint had it.

The clerk, unadventurous, had always wanted to travel, Now he was travelling, shanghaied.

The ransom money was now in Flint's safe. It was a fair return, he thought, for all the trouble and damage caused by Angelo.

"What about Angelo?" asked Horace, who was peeling potatoes for the evening meal.

"Send him back to Solly," snapped Jim. "This whole thing is sour."

"What about Solly?" asked Milky Waye. "He could make trouble."

"He should pick more trustworthy servants," said Flint. "We'll take the boy off in the car about midnight and drop him somewhere on the road to London. After that we'd all better take a holiday for a while—till Solly cools down."

"I was beginning to like it here," said Horace. "Minds me of old times. Except there aren't any trusties around, and there's something wrong with the wiring of the place. You know, Flint, you ought to get an electrician in and—" "Shut up," said Jim. "Why don't we cut the boy's throat and bury him in the rockery. Be a kindness to the world."

"The dog would dig him up and carry him home," said Milky. "Where's the whisky? We've got to think."

Flint produced a large decanter of whisky from the kitchen cupboard and they started to think.

When Angelo came down about an hour later to see what was happening about his supper, he found that they had done all their thinking and had passed out. The four of them were slumped unconscious around the kitchen table.

Angelo, whistling happily, made himself an omelette, pushed Jim O'Leary off his chair to the floor, and sat down to eat a leisurely meal. He was in no hurry. The knockout drops, which he always carried in his suitcase and which he had dropped into the whisky, were made from a special recipe of his father's. They would fix an elephant for an hour, a race horse for three hours, and any two-legged creature for a good six. Angelo had used one once on a boy film star from Hollywood who was scheduled to do a turn with him in a Royal Command performance. The boy had been out for two days and Angelo had given the show of his life.

When he had finished his supper, Angelo took Bugs into the garden and knocked off the heads of the remaining dwarfs. Then he came back and went through the pockets of the four men, taking their watches and wallets. In Flint's pocket he found a letter from the captain of the cargo ship, which had sailed that day from Southampton.

The letter interested Angelo very much. He took Flint's keys, went up to Flint's bedroom, and found his safe behind a water colour titled *A Distant View of Dartmoor*. Inside the safe was a brief case containing £39,800 in notes, and a brief scrawl from Solly which read, *What a wonderful scheme. Hope this will make all the boys happy.*

Angelo took the brief case, went back to the kitchen, and allowed himself an extra cigar and another gin and bitter lemon while he thought things over. All he had to do now—and he took his luck quite calmly—was to let himself out of the house with Flint's key and get back to London. He would hand the money over to his mother to bank for him. Then he could turn up at his hotel and say that three men, unknown to him, had dropped him on Waterloo Bridge.

There was nothing anyone would ever be able to do about it. The only thing he had to be careful about was to get to his mother without being recognized. He didn't want any copper picking him up with the brief case in his hand and hogging the glory for finding the kidnapped star and also poking his nose into the case and finding the money.

He decided to wait until midnight and then make for a main road, find an all-night café, and smuggle himself in the back of a London-bound truck. Trains were out—conductors were as nosey and glory-seeking as coppers.

Actually, it was a little after midnight when he left. At the last moment his sense of humour got the better of him. He spent a happy half-hour fixing false moustaches on the snoring four. And he painted Jim's nose red with garden paint. He also tied everyone's shoelaces together and reached inside their jackets and cut their suspenders or belts. For a while he had contemplated pouring treacle over their hair, but finally decided against it. Jim

O'Leary, for one, could easily be pushed over the line into violence, and Angelo didn't want his future marred by some act of berserk brutality in a dark alley.

So, just after midnight, Angelo, with Bugs at his heels, was on his way out of Brankfold and following a road which had been signposted Southampton 20 miles. Once he hit a main road it wouldn't be long before he found an all-night café. He took his time. The night was fine. He didn't mind how long it was before he reached London. When he got tired of carrying the brief case he handed it to Bugs who trotted along by his side carrying it proudly like any young dog which has learned a new trick.

The four men in the kitchen came back to life within a few minutes of each other. There was a great deal of groaning and stretching and muzzy shaking of heads.

Flint struggled to his feet, took a step forward, and fell flat on his face. Jim O'Leary followed him, repeated the act, and then, cursing, stood up and had his trousers concertina around his ankles. He let out a bellow of rage which brought Horace to life.

Horace stared blearily at Jim and then said, puzzled, "I didn't know you had a moustache, Jim. Been hitting the bottle, too, nose like a beacon—" He broke off as he tripped over his tied laces and crashed to the ground.

"That boy!" A great wail of anger came from Jim as he turned and caught sight of himself in the kitchen mirror on a cupboard door. Then:

"My wallet!" cried Milky.

"My watch!" roared Jim.

"Something wrong with my braces," said Horace.

"My flamin' keys"—this from Flint.

Then, as they sorted themselves out, a bellow of apprehension issued from Flint. Holding up his trousers, he stumped rapidly out of the room. While he was gone, Milky, the practical one, fished a length of clothesline from a cupboard and they fashioned belts for their trousers.

After a time Flint came back. He stood in the doorway and surveyed the company with a grim look on his rubicund face, and the sound of high-pressure seething escaped from between his lips—like a boiler about to blow.

"Gentlemen," he announced, "this is serious. The boy is gone."

"Thank God," sighed Jim.

"He's gone and he's taken forty thousand nicker of ransom money with him," said Flint. And then, as they looked amazed at him, he went on, "I know. Explanations are due."

"I'll say," said Milky. "You had the money all the time."

"I did. I was going to do a fair split with you all when the boy went back. That way Solly would think he'd lost all his money and we'd have racked up ten thousand each. It was practical common sense."

"Except," said Jim threateningly, "you'd never have told us if this hadn't happened. I ought to do you."

"But I thought the clerk chap had got the money," said Horace. "What about him?"

"Shut up," said Milky. "He's on his way to South America if I know Flint."

"Africa actually," said Flint. "But that's not the point. Angelo's flown with the money. We've got to get him."

Milky eased off his false moustache gingerly and said, "Let me think. He won't go to the police—not with all that money on him. He'll want to get it safely tucked away. His mother—that's it. She holds the moneybags for him. He'll want to get to her first before anyone picks him up. Which means?"

"What would you do?" asked Flint.

"What would we all do," said Jim. "It's obvious. He's on the road. Going to stow away on a lorry."

Horace said, "I still can't understand. I never passed out before."

They ignored him.

Ten minutes later they were all in Flint's car heading away from Brankfold on the only road which Angelo could have taken from the town. It was summer and already the sky was beginning to lighten. In another hour it would be full daylight.

Fortunately for them—or so it seemed—Angelo's progress had not been rapid. After a few miles he had developed a blister on his heel and was reduced to a slow hobble. Bugs now carried the brief case permanently and was getting tired of his duties.

They caught up with him after about half an hour on a long open stretch of road in open country. As the car pulled up alongside of him Angelo recognized them. He gave a whistle to Bugs to follow and slipped through the hedge. Forgetting his blister now, he put on a burst of speed which would have made his dog-thief father proud.

Flint said to Horace at the wheel of the car, "The road bends back at right angles a couple of miles up. You go on to the bend and wait for us. We'll follow him."

The three of them crashed through the hedge and were after Angelo in full cry. Horace, completely out of his depth, shook his head and drove on. Things were going too fast for him altogether. Meanwhile, Angelo and Bugs were streaking across the fields with the others in pursuit. It was a lovely morning for a hunt. Jim O'Leary led, going like the wind and with murder in his heart. Milky Waye followed him closely, wondering if he wasn't losing his financial grip, since he hadn't even thought of the double-cross which Flint had so nearly pulled off. And behind came Flint, stumping away on his wooden leg, and cursing.

Angelo kept up his speed for about five minutes and then began to slacken. Ahead of him he saw a range of farm buildings rise over the hedges. He found a field path and a few seconds later was in the farmyard. Knowing he could no longer rely on speed to save himself, he darted for a long low building, hoping to hide there while his pursuers went by.

With Bugs at his heels, Angelo raced to one of the buildings, jerked open the door, and leaped in. Immediately there was an explosion of white feathers and three hundred laying hens, disturbed at their breakfast, hit the ceiling and let out a cacophony of cackles which could be heard a mile away.

Angelo realized that his pursuers must have heard the noise, so he dashed through the building toward a door at the far end, knowing that he must look for a new hiding place. But the door was locked and bolted. Turning to go back to the other door, he saw Jim O'Leary come bursting in.

Angelo, ploughing his way through hens that would be egg-bound for a month from the shock, headed for a window on the far side of the house, pushed it open, and was through like a shot. Bugs followed him with a leap that was considerably hampered by the brief case he was still carrying. Angelo turned and slammed the window down on Jim's fingers as Jim grabbed at the sill.

Jim reeled back, letting out a scream of anguish that set the hens off again, and collapsed into a drinking trough. The next moment Milky Waye and Flint came charging into the building which now resembled a film set of a blizzard in an ascent of Mount Everest.

Jim leaped up, shouting, "Back to the door! Don't let the little bleeder get away!"

But as they turned to the door, they found it blocked by a man in breeches, tall and burly, angry-faced, a little egg around his lips from having been disturbed at breakfast, and holding a double-barrelled shotgun.

"A fine do, eh?" he roared. "The last time you come at night and pinch two dozen of my best hens. Now it's brazenfaced, daylight robbery. Ernie!" He shouted over his shoulder. "Get on the phone to the police—I'll hold 'em here!"

And he could, and he did. A twelve-bore shotgun was not to be treated lightly. The three—Flint, Jim, and Milky—stood panting, watching him, and slowly the hen house subsided to a quiet clucking and a few of the more phlegmatic hens made for their nest boxes to get on with the business of laying eggs that would, thanks to efficient marketing methods, be in the shops in four weeks' time marked *New Laid*.

Half a mile away Angelo saw a line of telegraph poles which marked a road. He headed for them, climbed a fence, and found himself in a large garden with a gravel path leading up to the doorway of a low red-tiled house.

As he approached, the door began to swing open. Knowing that he mustn't be recognized now that he had shaken off his pursuers, and aware that even in these bucolic depths his face was familiar, he jumped aside into a shrubbery and began to make a detour.

He didn't notice for a moment that Bugs was not following him. Bugs, bemused by recent events and tired out from carrying the brief case, headed straight on, up the path, and into the porch of the doorway. Here he was confronted by a portly, benign-faced gentleman with a clerical collar who looked down at him and said, "Well, bless my soul! A dog."

At this moment a hundred yards away Angelo discovered that Bugs was no longer with him. And it was at this moment that Angelo made his mistake. He gave a whistle for Bugs, low and piercing. But it was the wrong whistle out of the wide repertoire taught him by his father. It shrilled through the morning, *Drop everything and come at once.*

Bugs did just that. He dropped the brief case at the old gentleman's feet, and with a bark of relief was away and after Angelo.

Five minutes later Angelo hit the main road only to find Horace waiting for him in the car. But Horace was a different cup of tea from the others.

Angelo climbed into the seat alongside him and said, "It's all right, Horace. Just drive me to London."

"London?"

"That's right. It's been arranged with the others." Angelo leaned back and opened the rear door for Bugs to jump in.

"It don't seem right," said Horace.

"That's what they said," said Angelo. "Just drive me to London."

Horace shrugged. He'd never been the mastermind in any job, just a muscle man. He was used to doing as he was told. So he started to drive Angelo to London and after a few miles Angelo discovered that Bugs no longer had the brief case. He was pretty upset about this, but he kept it to himself, imagining that Bugs had dropped it in the chicken house. Anyway, he consoled himself, he had enough on Solly over this phoney kidnapping to blackmail him into a handsome payment for keeping his tiny mouth shut.

Somewhere in the suburbs of London, nearing lunchtime, Angelo and Bugs began to get hungry. Angelo made Horace stop the car outside a café, and leaving Bugs with Horace, Angelo went in to buy some biscuits and sandwiches. As he came to the door to return to the car, he saw that a motorcycle policeman had drawn up alongside Horace and Bugs. An interesting conversation was going on, if a little one-sided.

"Nice to see you, Horace," said the policeman. "Thought you was still inside."

"No, I ain't."

"Nice dog you got there. Nice collar too—gold with diamonds stuck in it. Up to your old tricks, eh?"

"What do you mean?"

"As though you don't know. This here is Prince Narrowmeath of Moortown."

"You're off your rocker," said Horace. "It's a dog, not a prince."

"Don't get funny with me, Horace. I can see it's a dog. And it was lifted from the Leroy Hotel. Brazen, you are.

Now then, just you follow me down the road to the station and we'll sort it out. Dog snatching, eh? A bit out of your line, isn't it? Still ..."

At this point Angelo withdrew into the café and made for the back door.

Well, there it is. Crime doesn't pay when a lot of rogues try to do one another down. A kind of rough justice operates. If you really want to make it pay you must go after law-abiding types who aren't used to jungle warfare,

Solly Badrubal lost forty thousand quid, plus another five he had to pay to Angelo to keep his mouth shut. He went out of films for four years and Angelo got a bigger contract with another company.

Horace got four months, and the other three, although their sentences weren't long, had a bad time in the Minerva Club when they came out for being such mugs as to be caught henlifting!

The only person who was really happy was the vicar at whose feet Bugs had dropped the brief case. He took it back into the breakfast room, opened it up, helped himself to a cup of coffee, and then with a great beam on his face turned to his wife and said, "You know, my dear, it is a wonderful world. A world of miracles. Here I have been for years and years trying to raise money for my Church Youth Camps and suddenly all I want is dropped on my doorstep by a dog."

"A dog, my dear?"

"An exceptional dog, of course, my love. Owned obviously by someone of great wealth. It had a gold collar with some kind of precious stones decorating it. The dog dropped the money at my feet and then, distantly, I heard its owner whistle, and away it went. So romantic, so generous! And obviously he wished to remain anonymous. But with the money was a note which made his intention clear. Listen to it. *What a wonderful scheme. Hope this will make all the boys happy.* Oh, it will, it will. Bless him."

A Stroke of Genius

The Minerva Club, in a discreet turning off Brook Street, is one of the most exclusive clubs in London. Members must have served at least two years in one of Her Majesty's Prisons and be able to pay £50 a year dues. In the quiet of its Smoking Room, under the mild eye of Milky Waye, the club secretary, some of the most ambitious schemes for money-making, allied of course with evasion of the law, have been worked out. But, although notoriety is a common quality among members, fame—real honest solid fame—has come to few of them.

Lancelot Pike is one of these few but, although he is still a member, he is not often seen in the august halls of the Minerva. However, over the fireplace in the Smoking Room, hangs one of his greatest works—never seen by the general public—a full assembly, in oils, of the Management Committee of the club; it shows thirty figures of men whose photographs and fingerprints are cherished lovingly by Scotland Yard.

Lancelot's road to fame was a devious one and the first step was taken on the day that Horace Head, leaning against a lamppost in the Old Kent Road and reading the racing edition, saw Miss Nancy Reeves. Without thinking, Horace began to follow her, some dim but undeniable impulse of the heart leading him. And, naturally, Lancelot Pike, who was leaning against the other side of the lamppost, followed Horace, because he was Horace's manager and was not letting Horace out of his sight.

Horace Head at this time was at the peak of his brief career as a professional middleweight fighter. He was younger then, of course, but still a wooden-headed, slow-thinking fellow with an engaging smile bracketed by cauliflower ears. He was wearing a grey suit with a thick red line in it, a blue shirt, a yellow bow tie, and brown shoes that squeaked.

He squeaked away after Miss Nancy Reeves and there wasn't any real reason why he should not have done so. She was a trim slim blonde with blue eyes and a pink and white complexion that made Horace think—and this will show how stirred up he was—of blue skies seen through a lacing of cherry blossoms. It had been a good many years since Horace had seen real cherry blossoms too.

Lancelot Pike followed him. Lancelot was a tall, slim, handsome, versatile number, with a ready tongue, a fast mind, and a determination to have an overstuffed bank account before he was thirty no matter what he had to do to get it. At the moment, Horace—at one fight a month—was his stake money.

If Miss Nancy Reeves knew that she was being followed, she showed no signs of it. She eventually went up the steps of the neighbourhood Art School and disappeared through its doors.

Horace continued to follow. He was stopped inside by an attendant who said, "You a student?"

Horace said, "Do I have to be?"

"To come in here, yes," said the attendant.

"Who," said Horace, "is the poppet in the green coat with blonde hair?" He nodded to where Miss Nancy Reeves was almost out of sight up a wide flight of stairs.

"That," said the attendant, "is Miss Nancy Reeves."

"She a student?" asked Horace.

"No," said the attendant. "She's one of the art teachers. Life class."

"Then make me a student in the life class," said Horace, the romantic impulse in him growing.

At this moment Lancelot Pike intervened. "What the devil are you after, Horace? You couldn't paint a white stripe down the middle of the road. Besides, do you know what a life class is?"

"No," said Horace.

"Naked women. Maybe, men, too. You've got to paint them."

"To be near her," said Horace, "I'll paint anybody, the Queen of Sheba or the Prime Minister, black all over. I got to do it, Lance. I got this sort of pain right under my heart suddenly."

"You need bicarbonate of soda," said the attendant.

Horace looked at him, reached out, and lifted him clear of the ground by the collar of his jacket and said, "Make me a student."

Well, it had to be. There was no stopping Horace. Lancelot helped to fill out the form and, in a way, he was glad because he knew that the classes would keep Horace away from the pubs between training. Horace was the kind who developed an enormous thirst as soon as training was finished.

So Horace became a student in the life class. It was a bit of a shock to him at first. He came from a decent family of safe crackers, hold-up men, and pickpockets. He didn't approve of naked women posing on a stand while a lot of people sat round painting them.

To do him credit, Horace seldom looked at the models. He sat behind his easel and looked most of the time at Nancy Reeves. Naturally he did very little painting—but he saw a lot of Nancy Reeves.

She was a nice girl. She soon realized that Horace was almost pure bone from the shoulders up; but she was a great believer in the releasing power of art, and she was convinced that Horace would never have joined the class if there had not been some deep-buried longing in him for expression.

Now Horace, of course, had not the faintest talent for drawing or painting; but, realizing that he could not sit in the class and do nothing, he would just smack an occasional daub of paint on his canvas in a way that loosely conformed to the naked shape of the model before him. Nancy Reeves soon decided that Horace was—if he was going to be anything—an abstract painter. She would come and stand behind him at times and her talk went straight over his head—but Horace enjoyed every moment of it.

After two weeks of this, Horace finally got to the point of asking her if she would go to a dance with him. Surprisingly, she agreed, and she enjoyed it because, whatever else he was not, Horace was quick on his feet at that time and a good dancer.

Now, a week after the dance, Horace and Lancelot had fixed up a little private business which Lancelot had carefully planned for some time. This was to grab the payroll bag of a local building firm when the messenger came out of the bank on a Friday morning.

Lancelot Pike had the whole thing worked out to the dot. Horace would sit in the car outside the bank, and Lancelot would grab the moneybag as the man came to the bottom of the steps and they would be away before anyone could make a move to stop them. It was a bit crude, but it had the merit of simple directness and nine times out of ten—if you read your papers—it works.

It worked this time—except for one thing. The man came down the steps carrying the bag, Lancelot grabbed it and jumped into the car, and Horace started away; but at that moment the messenger shoved his hand through the rear window and fired at Lancelot Pike.

But the gun wasn't an ordinary one. It was a dye gun full of a vivid purple stain. The charge got Lancelot full on the right side of the face, ran down his neck, and ruined a good suit and a silk shirt.

Well, there it was. They got back to the Head house, where Lancelot had a room, without any trouble from the police. Lancelot nipped inside with the moneybag and Horace drove off to ditch the car.

When Horace returned he found Lancelot hanging over the wash basin trying to get the dye off. But it wouldn't budge. It was a good rich purple dye that meant to stay until time slowly erased it.

"You won't be able to go out for a while," said Horace. "Months, maybe. The police will be looking for a purple-faced man."

"Lovely," said Lancelot savagely. "So I'm a hermit. Stuck here for weeks. You know what that's going to do to a gregarious person like me?"

Horace shook his head. He didn't know what a gregarious person was.

"We got the money," he said.

"And can't spend it. Can't put it to work to make more. Cooped up like a prisoner in the Tower. Me, Lancelot Pike, who lives for colour, movement, people, the big pageant of life, and golden opportunities waiting to be seized."

"I could go to the chemist and ask him if he's got anything to take it off," suggested Horace.

"And have him go to the police once he's read the story in the evening newspaper!"

"I see what you mean," said Horace.

So Lancelot—very bad-tempered—was confined to his room. For the first few days he kept Horace busy running to and from the public library getting books for him. Lancelot was a talented, not far from cultured type—things came easily to him and idleness was like a poison in his blood that has to be worked out of his system. But it was people and movement that he missed. Every evening Horace had to recount to him all that he had done during the day and, particularly, how he was getting on with Miss Nancy Reeves at the Art School.

Curiously enough, Horace was getting on very well with her. There was something simple, earthy, and engagingly wooden about Horace which had begun to appeal to Nancy Reeves. It happens that way—like calling to unlike ... think of the number of men, ugly as all get-out, with beautiful wives, or of dumb women trailing around with top intellects.

Anyway, Lancelot began to take a great interest in Horace's romance, and he knew that the time would come when Horace would ask the girl to marry him, and he was offering ten to four that she would not accept.

Horace wouldn't take the bet, but he was annoyed that Lancelot should think he had such a poor chance.

"What's wrong with me?" he asked.

"Nothing," said Lancelot, "except that you really aren't her type. To her you're just a big ape she's trying to educate."

"You calling me a big ape?"

"Figuratively, not literally."

"What does that mean?"

"That you don't have to knock my head off for an imagined insult."

"I see."

"I wonder," said Lancelot. "However, forget it. You ask her and see what answer you'll get."

Meanwhile Lancelot helped Horace with his homework from the Art School.

Each week each student did a home study composition on any subject he liked to choose. Lancelot got hold of canvas and paints and went to work for Horace. And then the painting bug hit him—and hit him hard.

He gave up reading books and papers, gave up listening to the radio and watching television, and just painted. It became a mania with him in his enforced seclusion—and it turned out that he was good. He had a kind of rugged, primitive quality, with just a lick of sophistication here and there which really made you stop and look.

Naturally, Nancy Reeves noticed the great improvement in Horace's work and her spirit expanded with delight at the thought that she was drawing from the mahogany depths of Horace's mind a flowering of his true personality and soul. There's nothing a woman likes more than to make a man over. They're great ones for improving on the original model.

Well, one week when Lancelot's face had faded to a pale lilac, Horace came back from the Art School saying that the home study that week had to be 'The Head of a Friend', and Lancelot said,

"Leave it to me, Horace. Self-portrait by Rubens. Selfportrait by Van Gogh—"

"It's got to be a friend," said Horace. "I don't know no Rubens—"

"Quiet," said Lancelot, and he began to ferret for a canvas in the pile Horace had bought for him. As he set it up and fixed a mirror so that he could see himself in it, he went on, "How's tricks with the delicious Nancy?"

"Today," said Horace, "I asked her to marry me. A couple more good fights and with my share of the wages snatch, I can fix up the furniture and a flat."

"And what did she say?"

"She got to think it over. Something about it being a big decision, a reckonable step."

"Irrevocable step."

"That's it. That's what she said."

"Means she don't believe in divorce. If she says Yes, which she won't, you'll have her for life. When do you get your answer?"

"End of the week."

"Twenty to one she says No."

"You've lengthened the odds," said Horace, wounded.

"Why not? Deep knowledge of women. When they want time, there's doubt. Where there's doubt with a woman, there's no desire."

"Why should she have doubts? What's wrong with me?"

"You're always asking that," said Lancelot. "Some day somebody is going to be fool enough to tell you. Horace, face it—you're no Romeo like me. I've got the face for it."

"I love her," said Horace. "That's enough for any woman."

Lancelot rolled his eyes. "That anyone could be so simple! A man who has only love to offer is in the ring with a glass jaw. Now then, let's see." He studied himself in the mirror. "I think I'll paint it full face, kind of serious but with a little twinkle, man of the world, knowing, but full of heart."

Well, by the end of the week the self-portrait was finished and Horace took it along to the school. He set it up on the easel and pretended to be putting a few finishing touches to it. When Nancy Reeves saw it she was enraptured.

"It ain't," said Horace, who had learned enough by now to play along with art talk to some extent, "quite finished. It needs a something—a point of ... well, of something."

"Yes, perhaps it does, Horace. But you'll get it."

She put a hand gently on his shoulder. They were in a secluded part of the room. "By the way, I've come to a decision about your proposal. It's better for me to tell you here in public because it will keep it on a calm, sane, level basis—a perfect understanding between two adult people who considered carefully, very carefully, before making an important decision. I feel that by producing in you this wonderful flowering of talent that I've completed my role, that I have no more to give. Marriage after this would be an anticlimax, since my attachment to you is really an intellectual and artistic one, rather than any warm, passionate, romantic craving. I know that you will understand perfectly, dear Horace."

"You mean, no go?" asked Horace.

Nancy nodded gently. "I'm sorry. But for a woman, love must be an immediate thing. There must be something about a man's face that is instantly compelling. Now take this painting of yours—there's a man's face that is full of the promise of romance, of tenderness and yet manly strength. I'd like to meet your friend."

For a moment Horace sat there, the great fire of his love just a handful of wet ashes. That Nancy Reeves could go for Lancelot just by seeing his portrait filled Horace with bitterness—a bitterness made even blacker by the fact that Horace had taken Lancelot's bet at twenty to one, and now stood to lose £100.

"You mean," said Horace, "that you could go for him?"

"He's certainly got a magic. You've caught his compulsive personality and—"

"You should really see him," said Horace jealously. "One half of his face is as purple as a baboon's—well, like this—"

In a fit of pique, Horace picked up his brush, squirted some purple paint onto his palette, and slapped the purple thickly over the right side of Lancelot's face.

From behind him Nancy Reeves's voice said breathlessly, "But Horace—that's just the defiant abstract touch it needed! The unconventional, the startling, the emphatic denial of realism … Horace, it's staggering! Pure genius. Don't do a thing more to it—not another stroke!"

Horace stood up, looked at her, and said, "There's a lot more I could do to it. But if you like it so much—keep him. Call it 'A Painter's Goodbye.'" He walked out and he never went back to Art School again.

A week later, while Horace was sitting dejectedly in Lancelot's room watching him work at a painting, the local Detective-Inspector and a Constable walked in unexpectedly.

The Inspector nodded affably and said, "Hello, Horace. Evening, Lance. Forging old masters, eh?" He was in a good mood.

Horace gave him a cold stare, and Lancelot kept his hand up to his face to cover his pale lilac cheek.

The Inspector went on, "Funny—I never connected you two with that wages snatch. Bit out of your line. Thought it was strictly an uptown job."

He leaned forward and looked at the painting on which Lancelot was working. "Nice. Nice brushwork. Fine handling of colour. Bit of a dabbler myself. Bitten by the bug, you know. Great relaxation. Go to all the exhibitions. They had one at the Art School yesterday. Picked up this little masterpiece by Horace Head."

The Constable stepped forward and brought from behind him Lancelot's self-portrait with Horace's purple-cheeked addition.

"Fine bit of work," said the Inspector. "Sort of neoimpressionistic with traces of non-objective emotionalism, calculated to shock the indifferent into attention. It did just that to me—so you can take your hand away from your cheek, Lance, and both of you come along with me."

And along they went—for a three year stretch.

But it didn't stop Lancelot painting. He did it in prison and he did it when he came out. Gets 500 guineas a canvas now, and his name is known all over the country.

But he's not often in the Minerva Club. His wife—who was a Miss Nancy Reeves—doesn't approve of the types there and rules the poor fellow with a rod of iron.

Three Heads are Better than One

While the Minerva Club certainly cannot claim to be the most respectable club in London, it is without doubt the most exclusive. Birth, rank, education, wealth, or sporting interests will get you into most clubs—but not into the Minerva. Its membership is limited to those who have served at least two years in one of Her Majesty's Prisons and who can, if elected, pay—no questions asked how—yearly dues of £50.

Honourable behaviour prevails inside, and no shop talk is allowed except in the smoking room after six o'clock in the evening. In this smoking room some of the cleverest criminal schemes have been devised by brains which, had they been directed to legitimate exploits, would have produced great captains of industry and successful politicians.

Only once has the decorum of the Minerva Club been disturbed and that was when some unknown guest stole the little gold statuette of the Goddess Minerva which used to stand on a small plinth outside the smoking-room door. The statuette was presented by one of the founder members, Maxy Martingale, famous in his day as a confidence man, to commemorate his selling of the Eros Statue in Piccadilly Circus. However, not all the members of the Club have the brilliance of a Martingale. Some—like the Head brothers—are just solid, hard-skulled citizens who do their best in the lower walks of criminal life.

Horace Head, once well-known as a pugilist, was a thickset, bone-headed man of about forty-five, with crisp grey hair and an engaging smile which split his broad face from cauliflower ear to cauliflower ear. His younger brother, Hubert Head, once a not quite so well-known pugilist, was also a thickset, bone-headed man, about forty-three, with crisp grey hair and an engaging smile. And his youngest brother, Harold, once a pugilist of even lesser renown, was a man of forty-one, thickset, bone-headed, with crisp grey hair and ... well, what does it really matter?

At this particular moment the three Head brothers were sitting in the smoking room of the Minerva Club, each with a large whisky in front of him, each considering the problem of their sister's wedding. Their sister was Marion Head who was a quiet-mannered, striking brunette of twenty-six, tall, beautifully proportioned, and the apple of her brothers' eyes.

This Marion, who beneath her quiet manner had a will of her own, had fallen in love with a member of the Minerva Club named Tony Risco. Tony was a dark-haired, self-contained, Latin-looking type who had a not inconsiderable reputation for forgery—a real artist and an educated man with the poise of an aristocrat. None of the Head brothers liked him, partly because— good Anglo-Saxon stock themselves—they distrusted all Latins, and partly because they seldom understood what he was talking about and, anyway, they thought he was a sissy.

The very idea of their sister married to Tony Risco made them squirm with inarticulate agony. They couldn't understand how Marion could have fallen for him. Horace had, in fact, once suggested that she should see a doctor. But Marion loved Tony, and Tony loved Marion, and the Head brothers were up against it, particularly Horace who, as the oldest, was the head of the family—Papa and Mama Head were long dead.

Horace took a long pull at his whisky and said, "I've done everything I can."

"Me, too," said Hubert.

"He won't rise," said Harold.

"Nothing in him," said Hubert.

"Be like punching a paper bag," said Horace.

What all this meant, of course, was that in order to break up the engagement the Head brothers had, in their limited way, tried to provoke Tony so that he could be frightened off. They had played tricks on him and insulted him in front of Marion— and Tony had taken it all with a smile.

They had once put a feather pillow under the hood of his car when he had taken Marion out for a drive—but he wouldn't be smoked off. They'd put buckets of water above doorways for him, pinned insulting labels on the back of his coat unknown to him, made him sit in trick chairs, doctored his drinks—in fact, pulled all the corny practical jokes they could think of; and the only reaction from Tony had been dignified and mildly reproving monologues which went completely over their heads.

Tony had stuck to Marion, and Marion had finally fixed the date of the wedding, and at a time when the Head brothers were hard put to find £10 between them, had informed them that they were responsible— particularly Horace, as head of the family—for the cost of her wedding. She wanted a wedding dress, a trousseau, a reception—complete with wedding cake and champagne—in the Ladies' Annexe of the Club, and they'd better get busy about it.

"She means it, you know," said Horace.

"She does," said Hubert.

"That she does," said Harold,

"We've got to face it," said Horace. "She's going to get hitched to that spineless wonder."

"Remember Ma?" said Hubert. "She's just like her. Once she makes up her mind, there's no shifting her."

"That's right," said Harold.

"Okay, then," said Horace. "If she's going to do it, then we've got to see her right. Wedding dress, trousseau—what's that?"

"Sheets and things for the bed, I think," said Hubert.

"No, underclothes," said Harold. "Knickers and bras."

"All right, then," said Horace. "You know about them, so you take care of them, Harold."

"Legit?" asked Harold.

"How can you without money?" said Horace. "You just do it and don't get caught. Hubert—"

"Okay. I know where there's some champagne. Got a friend who's a docker. Always unloading the stuff. How many dozen?"

Horace thought, then said, "Be about a hundred and twenty people here. Half a bottle each. How many dozen is that?"

"Don't know," said Hubert. "Make it a bottle each, that's easier. Ten dozen. What about the cake?"

"Me," said Horace. "I'll have a look round. Milky Waye will let us have the rest on credit." Milky Waye was the Club Secretary.

And that was that—each Head slowly and deliberately set to his job. But let it be said that years of experience had given them a certain facility and assurance in this kind of thing. So long as nothing unexpected turned up, they were reasonably competent, It was the unexpected that always threw the Heads.

Hubert—the champagne—had the easiest job. The docker he knew had a boy of fifteen who was keen on the ring and Hubert promised twenty free lessons in the manly art in return for some co-operation, and the docker agreed,

"Ten dozen it is, Hubert. Vintage or non-vintage?"

"Just champagne," said Hubert. "The stuff that fizzes. For a wedding."

After that all Hubert did was to turn up at the docks when his friend was off-loading, take the wink when the lorry driver went off to the canteen, and then drive the vehicle to the back door of the Minerva Club, unload, and then abandon the lorry in the Edgware Road. Easy.

Harold's job was a little more complicated. First of all, he had to get the right size dress. Marion obliged with her measurements and he paid a preliminary visit to one of the big stores and looked over the dresses, getting the girl to show him the right size. He picked one out and made a note of its position on the rack. He did nothing about inspecting underwear or sheets, being a shy sort of man.

The next day at about four o'clock he turned up at the store in his old clothes, carrying a plumber's bag, and went to the Men's Room. It was the oldest trick in the world. Nobody questions a plumber in a big store. Somebody had sent for him to check the bowls, he said, and in he went, smoked a cigarette with the attendant, then disappeared into a cubicle and rattled his tools for a while.

The attendant poked his head in later to say that he was going off for his tea, and Harold said that he'd be gone by the time the attendant got back, but that it was a big job and he would return tomorrow. When the attendant came back, the cubicle door was locked and an OUT OF ORDER notice hung from the handle. Inside was Harold.

He stayed inside until the store locked up, and then, with darkness, he came out. He took the dress, made a random selection of sheets and underwear, bundled the whole lot up, and dropped it out of a back window to Horace who was waiting below with a lorry. Then Harold came down on a rope which he had carried in his plumber's bag. Easy.

But it wasn't so easy for Horace. He had to get a wedding cake. He scouted around for a few days examining the windows of high-class confectioners. In the end he found three, none of them too far from the Minerva Club; they all had cakes in their windows, beautiful three- and four-tiered jobs, iced, gleaming, with little wedding bells, cupids, the works. He didn't know which to settle on until he noticed that one shop was called Marko and Son, and that reminded him that years ago Sam Marko, long dead—son, Simon, now in charge—had once been a black marketeer during the war and had applied for membership of the Minerva

Club. But he'd only got an eighteen months' prison sentence behind him and had been turned down. From that moment Sam Marko had gone straight, built up a good business, and died a worthy citizen, his only regret that he had never been a Club member—this because the poker game at the Minerva was the best in town and Sam was crazy about poker. For old times' sake, he decided to take the Marko cake.

Horace was glad that he had chosen the Marko shop because it was the nearest to the Club. He broke into the back premises on a non-baking night, lifted the cake very gently from the window, draped a sheet over it, and walked out and down the street, breathing hard, but his hands steady. Like every other member of the Club he knew exactly what time the policemen in the neighbourhood walked their beats and of course he had timed it beautifully. So, except for the small matter of the bride's brothers stealing top hats and morning clothes, all the preparations for the wedding were complete.

It was a beautiful wedding. Horace gave the bride away, and Marion, he thought, looked far too good for Tony; and Tony, his tanned face smiling with joy, led her down the aisle. Off they went to the reception at the Club.

The Annexe was crowded with club members and guests, and the champagne went round and round until it began to look as though a bottle a head was not going to be enough.

Then came the cutting-of-the-cake ceremony and Tony, one lean brown hand over Marion's, helped her to make the first cut. But as they both pressed down on the knife, the surface of the cake resisted their efforts. Tony, his Latin temperament stirring at this obstacle, held Marion's hand more firmly—but still the cake would not give.

"Maybe," said Horace, "it is a little stale from being in that window."

"Maybe," said Hubert.

"Or the knife is blunt," said Harold.

But at this moment Tony gave the lower tier of the cake a rap with the handle of the knife. In the silence of the room, watched by a hundred and twenty pairs of eyes, the cake echoed hollowly.

Suddenly Tony turned from Marion and faced the three brothers. As a murmur spread through the crowd, he held up his hand for silence. Then in a calm, even voice, full of control, but vibrant with growing passion, he addressed the three brothers.

"I have something of major importance to say," said Tony. "I address myself to my three brothers-in-law and crave the indulgence of the guests here for intruding a purely family matter into this happy atmosphere. For two years I have honestly, passionately, and worthily wooed Marion. And for two years I have borne with complacency and, I trust, dignity, the insults and the moronic practical jokes of my brothers-in-law, all designed to destroy the true love between Marion and myself. This—" his hand gestured toward the cake, "—is their last and final insult. Instead of a proper wedding cake, they have presented us with a plaster of Paris model, But let no one think that this final humiliation will, like the others, go unpunished

"What," said Horace, "is he talking about?"

"Your cake, I think," said Hubert.

"It ain't real," said Harold. "Just a phoney window display."

"Until now," Tony went on, "'I have stayed my hand, since it would not have been becoming for a suitor to assault— no matter what the provocation—the brothers of his fiancée, But now, since I am a member of the family, there can be no such prohibition. Family members are entitled to fight among themselves. Harold, I will take you first."

Tony stepped toward the three brothers. For a moment Harold's eyes were dull with puzzlement. Then a joyful light flashed in them.

"You mean, you want to mix it, Tony?" he asked happily.

"I do," said Tony.

And he did, and it was a revelation to the other two brothers. Harold squared up, a space was made around there, and then Tony dived in. It was like lightning hitting a rotten elm. Before Harold knew what had hit him he was on the floor, taking little more interest in the immediate proceedings.

102

"Nice footwork," said Horace appreciatively.

"But he leaves himself wide open," said Hubert. "My turn, I believe, Tony?"

"Yours," said Tony.

This time it took a little longer—say, twenty seconds—and Hubert joined Harold on the floor. A cheer rose from the assembled guests. This, as Solly Badrubal said afterward, was a wedding to remember.

Looking down at his two brothers, Horace shook his head.

"I'd never have believed it,. He grinned with delight. "You know how to handle yourself. Why, it's a treat to see but they're both a bit rusty. Now then, see what you can do against the head of the Heads."

And Tony showed him. It took five minutes and Horace put all he knew of his old craft into it, and the furniture and furnishings of the Annexe suffered badly. But Tony was like a flicker of lightning and, finally, it was Tony going in and out, bang, bang, and a beauty of an uppercut that laid Horace to rest with his brothers.

As they lay on the floor, Tony turned, lifted the cake, and threw it at their feet. The plaster of Paris model smashed into a thousand pieces, and the guests raised their glasses in a spontaneous toast, shouting with joy.

Tony turned to Marion, embraced her, and said, "I am sorry, my love, I should have been more restrained."

"Why?" said Marion, and her eyes shone with pride and devotion.

At this moment, as the three Head brothers began to sit up, Milky Waye came storming into the Annexe. He took one look around, and magisterial in his capacity as Secretary of the Club, addressed Tony and the three Heads.

"Gentlemen, may I draw your attention to Rule 136 of the Minerva Club bylaws? *Any members engaging in unseemly conduct, brawling, fighting, or such activities calculated to disturb the peace of other members and the good name of the Club are automatically, without trial or right of appeal, deprived of membership.* Gentlemen, you are no longer members of this Club."

Now, this was a thunderbolt—to be expelled from the Minerva Club was to be sent into the wilderness and never recalled. It could ruin the whole of one's professional life. The Head brothers gaped at Milky Waye, and Tony's face clouded as tragedy struck twice on his wedding day.

"Give over," said Horace. "It was just a family affair."

"No justification—you all know the rule," said Milky.

"Wait a minute, Milky," said Solly Badrubal. He had come over to the Head brothers and was standing, glass of champagne in hand, amid the wreckage of the cake, "There's another rule. Rule 25c, which reads: *None of the aforesaid rules of the Minerva Club shall be effective if, in the opinion of the Secretary and one other member of the Club, any offence, although proved, can also be shown to have materially benefited the Club."* He turned to Horace. "Where did you get this cake?"

"Sam—I mean, Simon—Marko's place," said Horace. "If I'd known—"

"Shut up," said Solly. He bent down and picked up something from the wreckage. "Just as I thought," he said, turning to Milky. "Remember old Sam Marko? Always wanted to be a member. Not a bad chap. Mad on poker. But he didn't have enough prison time to qualify. Often a guest here, round about the days when our statue of Minerva was stolen. Well, here it is."

He handed over a small gold statue of the Goddess Minerva which had been hidden in the plaster of the lower tier of the cake.

"Must have pinched it in anger, then didn't know what to do with it," said Solly. "So he hid it in his display cake and died without telling a soul. You can't say, Milky, that these gentlemen haven't materially benefited the Club. We've got our Minerva mascot back, haven't we?"

For a moment Milky hesitated. Then he said solemnly, "The point is well taken. Gentlemen, you are herewith reinstated."

And not only reinstated, but united, for from that moment the three Heads—now well aware of the true fighting calibre of their brother-in-law—were 100% behind Marion's husband.

"Just shows," said Horace, rubbing his jaw, "we was hasty about him."

"Never seen such footwork," said Hubert, tenderly fingering a swollen eye.

"Really packs a punch," said Harold, testing a loose tooth. The three of them raised their glasses to Tony.

Even for the Minerva Club it was "a wedding to remember".

Also Available

What's going on behind the doors of Fountain Inn?

When her employer suddenly disappears, young Grace Kirkstall finds herself accepting a new job at a new company in the same building – an oasis of tranquillity off the streets of London.

Ben and Helen Brown's startup company's pitch is that, for a small consideration, they will help people out of their major and minor fixes. Their first big commission initiates Ben into the gentle art of house-breaking, and Helen into the mysteries of the Society for Progressive Rehabilitation.

But for Grace, it will plunge her into more danger than she could ever have imagined...

Fountain Inn by Victor Canning

OUT NOW

Also Available

Mr Edgar Finchley, unmarried clerk, aged 45, is told to take a holiday for the first time in his life. He decides to go to the seaside. But Fate has other plans in store...

From his abduction by a cheerful crook, to his smuggling escapade off the south coast, the timid but plucky Mr Finchley is plunged into a series of the most astonishing and extraordinary adventures.

His rural adventure takes him gradually westward through the English countryside and back, via a smuggling yacht, to London.

Mr Finchley, Book 1

OUT NOW

About the early works of Victor Canning

Victor Canning had a runaway success with his first book, *Mr Finchley Discovers his England*, published in 1934, and lost no time in writing more. Up to the start of the Second World War he wrote seven such life-affirming novels.

Following the war, Canning went on to write over fifty more novels along with an abundance of short stories, plays and TV and radio scripts, gaining sophistication and later a darker note – but perhaps losing the exuberance that is the hallmark of his early work.

Early novels and story collections by Victor Canning –

Mr Finchley Discovers His England

Mr Finchley Goes to Paris

Mr Finchley Takes the Road

Polycarp's Progress

Fly Away Paul

Matthew Silverman

Fountain Inn

The Minerva Club

The Aberdyll Onion

Young Man on a Bicycle

About the Author

Victor Canning was a prolific writer throughout his career, which began young: he had sold several short stories by the age of nineteen and his first novel, *Mr Finchley Discovers His England* (1934) was published when he was twenty-three. It proved to be a runaway bestseller. Canning also wrote for children: his trilogy The Runaways was adapted for US children's television. Canning's later thrillers were darker and more complex than his earlier work and received further critical acclaim.

Note from the Publisher

To receive background material and updates on
further titles by Victor Canning, sign up at
farragobooks.com/canning-signup

Printed in Great Britain
by Amazon

18745506R00068